An Unexpected Spark Changes Everything

"I haven't swung a bat in ages," Duncan said. "Never was all that great at it, but I always loved to try. I can feel the blisters starting already. So, you in?"

Joel had that warm, solid feeling in his chest he got when he started something that was going to turn out good.

And damned if he hadn't earned a bit of relaxation.

"Okay, I'm in. I did my best with baseball, especially with my uncle as the coach. So you have to promise not to laugh at how bad I might be at it after all this time."

Duncan laughed, then covered his mouth with one hand.

"I'm sorry, that's not at you. I wasn't exactly an All Star. I don't think I'll get hit, but I have managed to get hit in a batting cage before. We'll have to promise not to laugh at each other. Deal?"

Joel held out one hand.

"Deal."

The contact between them hit like lightning.

Rippling, long-lasting, summer-night heat lightning.

Near Future Forward (with Jason A. Adams)

Dispatches from the Galaxy: A Space Opera Novella Trio

Dangerous Days on a Pleasure Planet

Storms of Future Past:

Dreaming the Storm

Joining the Storm

Into the Storm

Fighting the Storm

Storms of the Heart

Storms of Future Past Omnibus

Voices Through Time:

Songs in the Mountain

Secrets in the Land

Sorrows in the Earth

Walking the Ghosts

The Odd Society:

Independent by Means of Magic

Protected by Means of Magic

Collections:

Fantastic Shorts: Volume 1

Fantastic Shorts: Volume 2

Fantastic Shorts: Volume 3

Escape into Romance

Stepping Out of Reality

Facing Down Extraordinary

Hacking Cybercrime

Investigations Beyond Belief

Passages in the Real World

Fantastic Side Trips

A Kaleidoscope of Cat Tales

A Tapestry of Holiday Tales

Aunties Among Us

Four-Legged Heroes

Anthologies *with Jason A. Adams*:

Partners in Romance

Shadows Mountain Deep

Uncommon Holidays

Partnership in Crime

KARI KILGORE

THE COFFEE BOMB
and the
Corporate Spy

Spiral Publishing, Ltd.

For everyone who's indulged my love of batting cages
over the years

THE COFFEE BOMB
and the
Corporate Spy

1

The thing Joel Cabot wanted most in the world wasn't about to happen anytime soon.

Mainly because it seemed the entire planet would actually have to stop turning for a couple of days to give him a chance to slow down and take a breath.

His huge, three-sided desk was stacked from one end to the other with work requests, for one thing. On the long, black surfaces nearly surrounding him, piles of photos meant to inspire ideas for the all-important design of the official Grateful Grocer float for the fast-upcoming Rudolph County Harvest Festival and Parade took up almost every inch.

The grand event all of his coworkers—including the boss of them all—had made abundantly clear was by far the most important marketing and community relations opportunity of the year.

The stacks ranged from bright, full-color images ripped

out of magazines or printed off the internet, to hard-to-see black-and-whites on ordinary printer paper, to honest-to-goodness photographs that had been sent out and printed somewhere else, and years or even decades ago at that.

The kind of thing Joel most often saw in creaky, faux-leather-covered albums at his great-grandparents' houses. Even his grandparents had gone digital in the modern era of iPhones, Instagram, and Pinterest.

Scattered in with all the photos were hand-sketched mock-ups on yellow pages ripped out of legal notebooks, with ragged edges at the top of several to prove how much of a hurry the sketcher had been in. Most were quite good, really, using colored pencils that played strangely with the paper but got the point across.

His favorites were Rose-Bowl-Parade elaborate, as if a small Southern Illinois grocery store chain could somehow wrangle two or even three stories, or flat-screen televisions big enough to run the length of the float on both sides.

Well, maybe they could, but he wasn't about to suggest it.

Joel wasn't sure a few of the more imaginative and high-tech designs could be done even if money were no object. He had strong hints the budget for this project was sky high, but surely there were limits.

The rules of physics and the load-bearing capabilities of the regulation-sized float trailers the little town of Stidham, Illinois, was supplying to every local business had to be considered at some point.

Joel had added the stark, plain-paper printout of the official rules of the annual Most Fabulous Float in Rudolph

County contest himself, after enlarging it so anyone passing by should be able to read it if they cared to. He'd made sure to put it on the wall beside his desk once he realized just how overwhelming the inspiration tsunami was going to be.

The huge flatbed scanner, high-end photo printer, and a fancy iPad he used for drawing by hand had disappeared under the tidal wave of paper sometime the week before. Only the silvery metal arms holding two huge monitors up and out of the chaos kept them from getting buried as well. The keyboard attached to his laptop peeked out of the jumble for now, but he'd lost count of how many times he'd moved stacks off of it.

Joel would have sworn he still had coffee from his early morning fill-up, but the empty sunshine-yellow stainless-steel mug and world-class coffee breath convinced him he'd already drained his pre-lunch allotment.

From the huge picture window in front of him, he could see happy residents of Stidham going about their daily lives in the bright early August sunshine.

Strolling along the still-quaint main street, with vehicles swarming around diagonal parking spots like lazy bumblebees. All of them orbiting storefronts tucked into tan brick buildings that had stood there since a post-World War I building boom and still looked great over a hundred years later.

If Joel leaned far enough toward the glass, he could catch a glimpse of an even older town square with rows of flower beds maintained by local Girl Scout troops, and a decidedly old-fashioned green and white gazebo in the middle. The high-quality speakers tastefully hidden around the square made concerts, speeches, and evening movies quite impressive for such a small town.

Grateful Grocer was more than happy to donate to the square's upkeep, and to take the generous tax write-off on top of the eye-catching sign right beside the gazebo giving them plenty of credit.

All that old-school charm combined with a truly up-and-coming community that was sure to keep growing had drawn Joel back to much smaller-town living that he could have imagined when he fled another one not too terribly far away at eighteen.

He had what he would have called his dream job back in college, no arguing that. And being too busy rather than grubbing for piece work at a different office each day or trying to appear useful had to be a good problem to have, right?

The closest he could get right now was to close his laptop (helpfully supplied so he could work from home whenever duty or managerial whim required), silence his cell phone (paid for by Grateful Grocer, thereby making him always available), and stand up.

Stretch, and ignore the alarming crackling noise from several regions of his spine, which surely shouldn't be happening this often before he hit thirty.

Then retrieve his coffee mug from the paper and photo whirlpool so he could head to the break room for a refill, topped off with a quiet bit of sanity. All in the name of getting ready to meet his new assistant, who would miraculously arrive in time to help sort through the design nightmare and come up with something that would make the fewest possible people angry.

At least Joel hoped so.

And somehow get it all done before the October 15th deadline that now swooped through Joel's mind like a huge swarm of starving vultures, even when he slept.

A quick check to make sure he didn't look quite as rumpled and wrinkled as he felt. In other words, his normal work uniform of dark pants and undercover-nerd golf shirt hadn't taken on offensively deep ridges or valleys, and they hadn't picked up enough old photo dust or shreds of yellow paper to notice.

He'd have to go on faith that he hadn't scrubbed his frequently obstinate brown hair into anything resembling a porcupine, because he wasn't quite vain enough to keep a mirror at his desk or, gods forbid, snap a quick selfie to verify presentability.

Then he turned and crashed right into a man he'd never seen before.

"Oh, I'm so sorry! I didn't mean to sneak up on you like that!"

Joel managed to grab the edge of his desk without inciting an inspiration avalanche, already formulating his instinctive Midwest-nice apologies before he quite understood what had happened.

But getting a good look at the guy stopped all the mea-culpas before they made it from his brain to his mouth.

Because whoever he was, this man was an absolute stunner.

A little taller than his own not-quite six feet, with black hair that actually looked spiky on purpose, and in the best way possible. Amazing big brown eyes that were already crinkling at the edges to go with a megawatt smile.

All that and a slender yet muscular frame wearing a caramel-colored silk shirt that brought out the warm tones in his dark skin had Joel wondering how such a gorgeous creature could have possibly found his way to Small Town Central Illinois.

Much less the corporate headquarters of Grateful Grocers, not to mention his own overflowing desk.

"No need to apologize, I wasn't paying attention to a single thing around me. I'm Joel, the current resident of this dangerously messy corner. You looking for someone?"

The handsome man laughed with a voice deeper than Joel expected, in the very best way.

"I believe I'm looking for you, if you're Joel Cabot. I'm Duncan Jackson. Your new assistant."

Before his brain could issue the commandment to take a deep breath and play it cool, Joel's free hand decided to grab Duncan's arm.

"Oh thank the *gods* you're here, and yes, I know how over-the-top that sounds. But I'm about to drown in... Let me call them 'helpful suggestions' over here. That and at risk of succumbing to a major craving for caffeine."

Duncan grinned and swung his black messenger bag around to the front, then pulled out an impressively roomy coffee mug made of green steel.

"Right there with you. One of the first things I was going

to ask was the way to the break room. Want to go check it out now?"

Joel forced his hand to disengage from Duncan's nicely firm arm and smiled.

"Sounds perfect to me. Go ahead and drop your bag there behind my desk if you want. No one will see it behind Mount Check-Out-This-Great-Idea."

2

Duncan followed Joel into the nicest break room he'd ever seen, but he had to force himself to pay attention to his surroundings.

His eyes kept wanting to stray back to the handsome, charmingly desperate guy who'd knocked everything inside him for an unexpected loop with a simple, surely entirely non-romantic touch of the arm.

The round tables were standard enough shiny black, with deep red cushions on the chairs that matched the colors for Grateful Grocer stores, naturally. An impressive row of hanging plants by broad windows added a soothing touch of green, and in any other corporate break room, they would have added a fresh, clean scent to the space.

In this case, and befitting a growing grocery chain that punched far above its weight, the plants didn't stand a chance against the scrumptious aroma of good coffee, hot pastries just out of an actual oven, and a pepperoni pizza spinning on one of those dedicated pizza bakers Duncan had always wanted for himself.

A young woman wearing the same red-and-black uniform he'd seen in a Grateful Grocer store the day before—when he was doing background research for this job—smiled as she pulled out a tray of apple Danishes that added a heady hit of ginger and cinnamon.

Duncan ignored the rumbling in his stomach, but he couldn't help smiling himself when he realized the soft music in the background was the same gentle orchestral versions of pop songs played in the stores.

Tunes to shop by, and apparently at Grateful Grocer headquarters, to eat absurdly decadent food by.

But the real star of the show had to be a coffee bar as nice as anything he'd ever seen in a nice hotel or restaurant. He had his choice of several different brews in gleaming steel carafes, a fully loaded espresso machine, and cold brew displayed in a glass-fronted mini-fridge. Another fridge held all the milks and creamers the chain carried, and a few he'd never seen before.

He didn't bother looking at the full-sized refrigerators that surely contained an equally impressive variety of soda, tea, and overpriced bottled water.

Despite jumping at the chance to do a bit of small-time and silly undercover work for a rival small-town grocery chain —a fascinating break in the middle of his self-imposed down-time in a tough career that had gotten a bit too hectic and intense—Duncan had quite simple tastes when it came to caffeine.

Regular with a barely-there splash of cream would do him just fine.

And when it came to men, no amount of study and preparation beforehand could have warned him how well Joel Cabot would fit the bill.

It wasn't only the adorably rumpled hair, or the not-quite-standard-issue business casual uniform that flattered every last bit of his huggable, dead-sexy, broad-shouldered frame. Who else could get away with an apparently conservative, office-day print that was actually an uber-nerdy pattern featuring a series of tiny robots marching in opposite directions?

And even though he was there under entirely false pretenses of wanting to help organize the chaotic mess on Joel's desk, Duncan found himself truly inspired to winnow down those piles and get started.

Not because of a little paycheck or the incredibly goofy possibility of stealing Grateful Grocer's float design either. All that was nothing more than a way to distract himself and pass a little time, have a little fun, and make a little cash.

Amateur-hour stuff or not for Joel, the folks who'd hired him (again, under false pretenses) cared *very* much about getting that insider edge, partly because GG had won the contest six years running.

And their feud with the chain's owner, who they furiously proclaimed was a cutthroat only out to destroy longstanding local businesses no matter what it cost.

No, Duncan wanted to *comfort* Joel, to make him feel

better. To take a literal and metaphorical load off his shoulders, and maybe take him home and make him a cup of hot cocoa and a plate of chocolate chip cookies for good measure. Do whatever it took to coax another of those gorgeous smiles out into the open, and catch a glimpse of twinkling highlights in his amazing blue eyes.

In other words, not a single impulse that would help Duncan with this job, and many that would probably lead him down the road to more heartache that he had the mental or emotional bandwidth to deal with right now.

Time for a diversion, for himself if not for the target of this little gig. And maybe a quick bit of information gathering to get this whole situation underway and over with before he got himself into trouble.

"No wonder the recruiter said this is one of the best jobs in town," he said, waving his mug toward the Great Wall of Coffee. "I didn't even know half this stuff existed."

Joel rolled his eyes, but the knee-weakening smile made an appearance.

"Yeah, they tempt you in the door with offers of never having to pack a lunch or rush around and get gross takeout again, and I guess that's true." He glanced over at the pastry chef, but she had her head bent over the tray full of Danishes with a tiny bag of what looked like sparkly gold frosting in hand. He went on in a lower voice. "Once you're here, though, you realize all this is nothing but incentives to be at work as much as possible without the pesky temptations of going home much at all, or even getting out into the fresh air for half an hour. And on that cheery note, I truly am glad you're here.

So what made you decide to jump into the weirdly competitive grocery store float business?"

For the first time since he'd started walking the path of a professional spy-type when he was fresh out of college, Duncan hesitated to serve up the smooth lines he'd practiced to perfection before ever walking through the door.

Joel's face had a hopeful, almost innocent look that made Duncan feel like he was about to hand an extra-sour, hot-pepper-laced lollipop to an adoring toddler who'd been promised a sweet treat.

"It's kind of a sideways career change, really. I've worked with computers for ages, more on the operating systems and hardware side than getting to use them myself. From what I can tell, grocery stores use some really interesting stuff on that side with point-of-sale scanners and inventory and such, but I don't much want to work on that stuff now. Anyway, I've always thought graphic design was fascinating. Some of the things you create seem like magic to me. And most of the time, designers love what they do."

Now Joel's cheeks flushed so red Duncan was surprised he couldn't feel the heat against his own skin, which was a thought he was better off not having right then.

"I'm sorry, Duncan, I threw ice water on your ambitions before we had a chance to get to know each other. Here, let's grab some go-juice and sit down before the starving lunch crowd gets here. What's your favorite?"

Duncan shrugged, happy he could be completely honest about this part.

"Pretty simple, really. If the coffee's good, just a splash of something to lighten it up a tiny bit. I guess I'm low maintenance on that front if nowhere else. Or maybe I'm just stuck in a long, dreary rut and afraid to try something new, and with a lot more than caffeine."

He ducked his head, hoping his face didn't show his irritation at revealing a whole lot more truth than he'd meant to just then. Never mind that he was here to do a job. The habits of a long-term snoop, not to mention a normally private kind of guy, usually meant he didn't get around to that much sharing until well after dates turned into overnights.

And way too often, not even then.

With the kind of perfect timing that would have felt right at home in a great rom-com movie (that almost never featured gay characters, though they *totally* should), Joel glanced at the pastry table to make sure the chef's back was still to them, then put his own mug down and reached into another mini fridge. This one had a normal solid door instead of glass.

"Now this is absolutely top-secret," he nearly whispered, "and I'd end up with a lapful of trouble for showing you. But this is one of the coolest things Grateful Grocer has in the product development pipeline right now."

He held out his hand, palm down, and Duncan couldn't help holding his own out in return.

At least it kept him from wondering exactly what Joel with a lapful of trouble might look like.

And an ice-cold sphere dropped into his hand. A deep-brown sphere wrapped in a clear label with dancing coffee beans arranged in a pattern a lot like the robots on Joel's shirt.

It was perfectly round and much heavier than it looked, almost like it was made of metal.

"What is this? Feels like a coffee bomb."

Joel grinned like a little boy, making Duncan feel like a dirty old man even though he was actually a couple of years younger.

"That's pretty much what it is. Have you ever seen those little balls of tea that you drop into a cup of hot water and they unfold like a flower?" He wanted for Duncan to nod. "This isn't anywhere near as pretty, but it's kind of the same thing. Here."

Duncan happily handed his mug over, and watched as Joel pulled a tab he hadn't noticed. Joel slipped the coffee-bean-patterned cover off then rolled the coffee bomb inside.

"This wrap is biodegradable," Joel said. "It can go right into the compost or wherever you like, and it dissolves pretty fast. They're working on making one that melts right along with the coffee, but it's not quite there yet. Do you like hot or iced?"

"Usually hot, but since the air's like soup out there today, iced sounds delightful."

Joel carried the mug over to a huge, etched-glass water carafe on the counter.

"The highest quality drinking water, and available in our stores, of course. Even I have to admit it tastes great. Watch."

He pulled a little glass lever shaped like a raindrop back, sending a cascade of water into the mug.

Where it immediately turned the same rich, dark brown as the frozen ball.

"This one is straight up medium roast," Joel said, handing it to Duncan. "They're working on a bunch of different strengths, and with sweetener and creamer added in. The packaging design isn't quite there yet, obviously. Another item on my ever-expanding to-do list."

When Duncan took his mug back, he couldn't help closing his eyes at the intense coffee aroma that drifted his way.

"If this tastes anywhere near as great as it smells, these will sell out in no time. Do they have to be kept cold?"

Joel shook his head as he turned to grab another coffee bomb for himself.

"Nope, they do just fine in a box on the counter. Like you said, they wanted us to try these to match the weather. They're planning seasonal lines eventually, with flavors for holidays and everything. The obvious pumpkin spice apocalypse, and things like eggnog in December. Probably something gross and green for St. Patrick's Day. But I'm curious what they'll come up for Valentine's Day, Easter, and Halloween."

Duncan raised his mug to hide what he suspected was a much too obvious puzzled frown.

How did such a small grocery chain come up with the research and development budget for this? And did they really expect a bunch of frugal, practical Midwesterners to stock up on coffee bombs when they could grab the same old can of instant they and their parents and grandparents and beyond had grown up with?

He couldn't imagine his own nearby family making that choice for any amount of money or marketing.

Most of that vanished from his mind when he took his first drink of cold, perfectly balanced, bitter-and-chocolate-tinged ambrosia.

"My grandmother would have sworn she'd died and gone to *heaven* if she'd gotten a sip of this."

Joel turned his face just enough to the side to look irresistible and flirty, leaving Duncan as shaky in his belly as his knees.

3

Joel had his hands full with a lot more than his own still-frozen coffee, which he wasn't sure he needed at the moment. Not when he was already hyped up enough that he might start the over-caffeinated jitters before he had another drop.

Besides his absurd work overload, which was the real reason Duncan was here, he'd run his mouth to an alarming degree, empty break room or not.

Fussing about his job to a new employee, then showing off the strictly-inside-this-room-only coffee pucks on top of it all. Though he might be able to get away with that by giving Duncan credit for the potential name Coffee Bombs, which made a heck of a lot more sense than anything GG's marketing department had come up with so far.

He turned away and moved over to the hot water tap built

into the wall beside shelves full of a staggering variety of teas (many not sold in their stores at all), and filled his mug.

The earthy, dark aroma turned up his excitement all by itself.

"I had the feeling you'd dig the Coffee Bomb, which is a brilliant name for it. I'm going to suggest it to marketing, or maybe just mock up a label and show it to them if I can find the time. That would work a whole lot better than listening to a two-hour argument about the placement of every letter and sliver of space."

He picked up a bright yellow ceramic jar with bees all over it (one of the Grateful Grocer's top sellers) and tilted a drizzle of honey into his mug. Then he held it out toward Duncan with his eyebrows raised.

"You know, I normally take cream," Duncan said, "but this is too close to perfect to mess with. And I'm sorry to be so nosy when I just got here, but why would the marketing folks want to tinker with your designs that much, anyway?"

Joel took a sip, trying to buy himself a little bit of time before he started running at the mouth again. Reasonable enough question, even from a new employee. Kinda cheeky, sure, but that just played into the feeling of his hitting the assistant mega-jackpot.

"I'm gonna grab one of those Danishes, then we can talk? There's plenty in case you want one. It's a write-off, so they want us to gobble them up."

Duncan rolled his eyes, but he grinned at the same time.

"Thank you for the excuse. They smell amazing, and I

wasn't sure if I needed a certain number of hours on the job to qualify."

A few pleasantries with Kaylie, who was so dang good Joel never missed a chance to try whatever she made, and he and Duncan sat in the quietest corner of the break room. Pretty much against The Official Wall of Soothing Greenery.

Each of them now had an oval made of flaky, buttery pastry with golden apple filling piled high in the middle, with fabulous swirls of cinnamon icing that sparkled like real gold. Tucked onto cheery red plates exactly the right size and shape (always available in-store).

The scent alone was almost enough to distract Joel from Duncan's extremely good question, but not quite enough to make him forget how good-looking Duncan was.

"Okay, you asked me a perfectly reasonable question," Joel said. "And I intend to answer you. But I can't possibly let you miss your chance to try anything Kaylie makes while it's still warm. That would be a terrible way to welcome you to Grateful Grocer. So how about we dig in first?"

Duncan leaned forward and looked at Joel from under his eyebrows, somehow turning his charm up to at least thirteen.

"I was trying to figure out how I was going to manage to pay attention to a word you said with this gorgeous thing distracting me. We'll have plenty of time for other distractions after we eat."

Joel pretended his mind hadn't gone in about twenty extremely work-inappropriate directions, and focused on the luscious treat on his plate instead. He could only hope he'd managed to finish his at a pace somewhat slower than inhalation.

He wasn't sure either of them succeeded with that, but he didn't think either of them had crumbs in their hair or bits of apple on their faces in the end.

"Now that we've got the basic survival functions out of the way," he said, "at least when it comes to something that irresistible, I'll do my best with your question. The truth is the folks here are usually pretty good at letting me do my job. They've got more than enough to worry about with their own workloads."

"What else do they do? From what little I saw walking through, there are a ton of high-powered computers around here. Specialized stuff I've never seen before."

"So you have been paying attention to the IT side of things despite yourself." Joel winked so he wouldn't seem like too much of a smartass, and thankfully Duncan smiled. "They handle just about everything that happens at all the stores from here. Way more than I would have guessed before I started. The inventory is centralized, triggered by deliveries and what gets scanned through at checkout. People here can even tell which perishable items have been on the shelf too long and send out an alert."

"Wow. I thought all that stuff was local, but I guess I haven't seen anyone with those little machines putting prices on cans of soup since I was a kid. Probably keeps the store managers from drifting into *micro*managing, since that seems to all be handled from here too."

"Not as much as you'd think," Joel said, "since computers

handle it all. That kind of...obsessive micromanagement only really crops up with new product lines. And of course this damn parade. It's not a bad place to work."

Duncan swallowed the rest of his coffee without looking away from Joel's eyes.

"What *is* the deal with the parade? I haven't been in town for long, but I haven't heard anything about a big prize or anything like that."

Joel shook his head. "Not a cash prize if that's what you mean. It's more marketing."

He looked around the break room, but Kaylie had already arranged two trays full of her sinful delights and departed. She'd tucked the pepperoni pizza into a bright red quilted warming bag and set a cheese pizza to spinning toward perfection, but no one had wandered in to devour any of it yet.

"I think it comes down to bragging rights as far as our CEO is concerned," Joel said. "And on top of us winning several years in a row already, a whole bunch of people around the region have gotten to the point of... Well, I'll just say not everyone loves the way Grateful Grocer does business."

Duncan's thick-but-neat eyebrows lifted toward his black hair, but he looked more surprised than suspicious.

"Ohhhhh, the *best* kind of break room gossip, because it's most informative gossip for the new guy in town, too. Do tell. If you want to, I mean."

Now Duncan's mouth turned down, only for a second, before his expression went back to neutral handsome and interested. Enough to set up a faint tingle in Joel's belly that he couldn't say for sure was excitement or alarm.

But no one had asked him how he felt about work for so long he decided to brush it off.

Gossip was what break rooms were for, after all. And Duncan *was* new in town, and surely the neighborly thing would be to help him feel right at home.

"I imagine it's the same kind of thing that goes on everywhere when any kind of chain store really starts to take off," Joel said. "No one in the other small towns paid much attention when Ms. Vincent opened her first store a few years ago, or the second. Those were in places you couldn't quite call towns anyway, and they hadn't had any kind of grocery store since theirs closed down years ago. When she started buying old buildings in towns that *did* have local stores, though, and could offer the same things for less, people got fussy. You wouldn't believe the rumors and crazy stuff they come up with."

Joel wasn't about to admit it to Duncan or anyone besides himself, but he'd wondered a time or two how GG managed to grow so fast and still have enough money for all those new products.

Duncan nodded. "I've seen that with gas stations and hardware stores for sure. A big chain moves in, and the shops that have been there for years can't keep up. Shoppers never seem to mind the changes after a while, not if prices are better."

"That was part of it, yeah. At first. When Grateful Grocer started offering a bunch of specialty things that no other store could get at a reasonable price, some folks got kind of nasty about it. Things like this, and all kinds of other stuff." Joel waved toward the Danish-shaped plates in front of them. "Ms. Vincent has a knack for figuring out ways to keep the costs down, then turning the profits right back into something new. She's got plans for a bunch of new stores in bigger towns lined up, and a big product launch every quarter this year."

"Like these fabulous coffee bombs. Which are one of the best new things I've heard of for a long time, even if I wasn't supposed to know about them." Duncan let out an irresistible giggle, and the dancing tingles in Joel's belly went one-hundred-percent exhilaration. "Make that *because* I wasn't supposed to know about them, but you told me anyway."

The sound of chattering voices heading their way interrupted the supercharged atmosphere between them, and Joel settled on a balance between relieved and disappointed. Despite the slow-to-dismal state of his love life, jumping into a potentially uncomfortable situation on day one made absolutely no sense.

Certainly not when part of his recent hermit-like existence was because he so desperately needed an assistant.

"Tempting as it is to stay right here and keep talking," he said, "I suppose we should head back and get going before the piles on my desk start getting bigger all by themselves."

Duncan gave an exaggerated sigh and smiled at the same time.

"I guess that is why I'm here." He got up and gathered their plates and forks, then carefully arranged them in the stainless-steel heavy-duty dishwasher beside the big refrigerator. "I packed my lunch today, but I think I'll skip it tomorrow. That pizza smells incredible."

The usual group of caterers walked in just then, and the Southern gentleman who did most of the dough-wrangling for Grateful Grocer headquarters executed a quick bow without breaking stride.

"I thank you for saying so, young man. Be sure and drop back by for some of my garlic knots this afternoon."

"I sure will, sir," Duncan said, patting his flat tummy. "Otherwise I won't be able to concentrate on a thing for the rest of the day."

Joel waved toward the laughing crew as he followed Duncan out of the break room, already convinced he was going to get himself into trouble with his new assistant.

And looking forward to it a whole lot more than he should.

4

Duncan did his best to pay careful attention to Joel's explanations of the general workflow and expectations at Grateful Grocer, feeling more guilty by the minute about the real reason he was there.

He didn't even have to consider how much he already liked Joel to get there, either.

Considering the tidal wave of design suggestions—including several more that had been added to the top during their quick Danish break—was more than enough to stir up doubts all by itself.

One reason he was so good at the corporate spy game was his exceedingly organized nature. So add the fact that he was itching to get the mess sorted out and winnowed down into something useful, and he was more twitchy than extra coffee could begin to explain.

And closer than he'd ever been to walking out on a job before it even started.

Joel leaned back in his envy-inducing black ergonomic chair and rubbed his eyes, then made an adorable attempt to smooth his messy hair.

"So that's probably more than enough for you to decide to save yourself and run screaming. But I hope you'll feel like hanging around for a while, probably despite your better instincts."

Duncan decided to take a chance on telling the truth, at least part of it.

"My instincts get me into trouble more often than not. I'm too interested in seeing this whole float drama from the inside out to back out now. What can I do over the next few hours to make your job easier? Within reason, of course."

Joel raised one eyebrow. "You mean making all this mess disappear with a wave of your hand is off the table? Eh, I'll settle for having some kind of...order to it all. You know, some-thing simple like photos versus drawings versus printouts so faded I have no idea what they're even supposed to be."

Duncan nodded once and rubbed his hands on his thighs.

"Done. Will anyone mind if I make the mess a lot worse before it gets better? As in stacking piles on the floor so I can sort it out. Carefully, I might add. Some of these pictures have to be older than either one of us."

"Some of them are older than my parents. Most people who venture back here these days are trying to sneak so I won't catch them adding to the disaster of my workspace. I'm just thankful the ones who want their stuff back put their names on them, because I never would have had a chance to keep track. The rest we can toss when we're through."

Joel looked at the piles again with a rueful smile.

"Hardly anyone else is likely to bother until after the big parade," he said, "so pile away. In fact, just go with what makes sense to you and tell me where you want me to put things. I might *finally* learn to get better at this myself."

Duncan ducked his head and ordered his dirty mind to stop right where it was and not take one single step down the imaginary path that had just sprung into life inside his imagination.

Grabbing a handful of home-printed photographs and designating their spot on the red-and-blue-patterned carpet at least got him started on a useful distraction. Though his budding ideas of getting his clandestine job done without Joel ever finding out were most likely going to get him into more trouble rather than less.

The two of them had gotten one side of the huge desk cleared by the time someone finally made their way back to the graphic design corner. And Duncan realized this fun little time-passing gig was about to get more interesting than he'd bargained for.

"Looks like you two are making serious progress!" an oddly threatening yet cheerful voice exclaimed, making the two of them jump.

Duncan turned to see a sharp-eyed woman *lurking* a few steps away from Joel's desk—there really was no other word for the way she'd sneaked in and stood halfway behind one of the low cubicle partitions even in a brightly lit room.

Her 1990s-blonde-with-brown-roots hair was cut shaggy chin-length, and her obviously expensive but trendy golf shirt and pants make her look like she'd just stepped out of a golf warehouse with a stack of easily coordinated outfits in a bag covered with brand logos. Her old-fashioned color-block golf shoes (presumably without the spikes) picked up the lime-green collar accents on her shirt.

Dressed to impress, small-town-business-owner style.

Not all that different from the clients Duncan had worked for over the years, or from the corporate types he met on his investigative jobs. The fact that she smiled rather than frowning or scowling set her apart from most of them, at least in the *appearance* of friendliness.

But between the hard edge to her smile and the tension he sensed from Joel, Duncan's guard went up immediately.

"Just getting things organized." Joel got up from the carpet and brushed at his knees. "This is Duncan Jackson, my rescuer when it comes to digging down to the top of my desk. Duncan, meet Bonnie Vincent. The founder and CEO of Grateful Grocer."

Bonnie strode forward and grabbed Duncan's hand while he was halfway through standing, giving it a squeeze and two hard shakes. She let go, stepped barely over the line into too close, and aimed a rapid stream of words at his face.

"Glad to have you aboard, Duncan. Joel normally does a great job keeping up with everything we need, but I'm afraid this time of year gets overwhelming for everyone. If anyone around this place needs the help, it's him. Got any questions for me, or need anything?"

"I'm fine so far, thank you. Joel and I were just getting all these great ideas for the big float sorted and put into order. He's got a heck of a lot to choose from."

She oozed sideways into Joel's space and slapped him on the shoulder.

"Well, he knows just how important this whole project is to the Grateful Grocer family, don't you, Joel? We really do arrange our whole year around it. Marketing, product launches, community outreach, the works. You *might* even say our float for the Harvest Festival and Parade is one of the main reasons we finally managed to fit such a talented graphic designer as Joel into our budget last year."

Joel's chest rose and fell in a silent sigh before he answered.

"I hope I do the job right for all of you, Ms. Vincent. And I hope I'll get a chance to talk to the float committee about what they can do before it's time to lock any designs down. I'd hate to give them something that's too hard or impossible to put together. Things like this can be easy to draw, maybe not so easy to build."

Ms. Vincent shook her head, smiling the whole time.

"Now don't you worry yourself about that, Joel. Focus yourself on making it look fantastic and leave that part to the committee, and to me. You might be surprised at what we can get done."

"Will do. And I certainly appreciate having Duncan here to help keep everything on track."

Bonnie made a show of leaning forward to peer at the stacks on the floor before she tapped on the recently cleared side of the desk with short nails painted a shiny red that matched Grateful Grocer's colors.

Duncan hadn't realized the desk's top was a groovy, old-school kind of burgundy until they'd moved the bottom layer out of the way.

"You've got a good start," Bonnie said, "at least when it comes to winning the neatest desk award. I'll have to get Joel to design that when we get around to offering one. Make me proud, boys. Make me proud."

She dropped a not-at-all-creepy-but-still-disturbing wink, turned on the heel of her unmissable shoes (definitely without the spikes since the carpet survived), and walked away.

Joel let out a properly loud sigh this time and lowered his chin toward his chest for a long few seconds.

"She's...very dedicated to growing the stores," he said, looking up at Duncan. "Comes across as a little brusque sometimes."

Duncan took his time answering instead of letting the first words to pop into his mind escape through his mouth. Brusque or even short or rude was one thing, and a certain level of *pushing* was part of the game when it came to a growing business.

Bonnie Vincent struck him as a lot closer to manipulative and downright vicious behind her overly bright smile.

And something in her manner sent him right back to wondering where the hell a company this size came up with the cash to grow so quickly, much less the research and development money it would take to launch new products at all.

"I guess that explains why everyone is so invested in this

float thing, too," he said. "If the boss thinks it's the biggest deal of the year, no one wants to argue. All the more reason for me to do everything I can to help you. I hope I'm not out of line if I say she's kind of…intense."

Joel tried to resist for a few seconds, full lips twitching and curving into a smile, then he let out an irresistible giggle.

"That's a generous way to put it, and you're not even a little bit out of line. Think we can get these piles off the floor so we can go to lunch? Or will it all magically recombine itself and get even worse?"

Now it was Duncan's turn to grin.

He forced his deepening curiosity about Ms. Vincent and how she was bankrolling Grateful Grocer to the back of his mind. He had time to dig into that later if he decided to, after he got the scoop on the big fancy float.

That thought went to the back of his mind too as soon as he looked into Joel's eyes.

Joel who was already trusting him, and depending on him. And who would absolutely get blamed if the top-secret final design got out into enemy hands.

"I think we can keep the piles far enough apart so they won't reproduce," he said. "While we're at lunch, anyway. I *would* suggest a bigger separation between them for overnight if you don't want to come back to your whole office stacked neck deep. Now let's get out of here before she comes back."

5

The rest of the afternoon evaporated in the kind of high-productivity haze Joel hadn't experienced since before the first stack of Fabulous Float Follies landed on his desk.

Duncan helped him get all the *suggestions* wrangled and organized faster than Joel could have done a quarter of the work. And the way Duncan sorted them was entirely genius.

The biggest pile—thank all the gods of marketing and accounting—was for ideas too elaborate or too expensive to consider. Joel wasn't sure that was possible at first, not with Ms. Vincent's always impressive budget for everything under the sun.

And her not-so-subtle hints about how vital the float was to that budget continuing to grow.

But Duncan's clear-eyed assessment of things that were impossible in small-town Southern Illinois in the time they had—with *any* budget—made too much sense to resist. And clearing out *impossible* let Joel finally begin to get his head around *doable*.

The first step to eventually landing on appropriate, cool-yet-impressive, and hopefully clever enough to win this ridiculous and fiercely fought contest.

Whether he wanted to admit it or not, right then Joel was better suited to sorting and arranging that he would have been at actual design work, partly because kneeling on the floor with Duncan had him distracted and giggly.

Combined with their lunchtime gabfest, Joel found himself a lot closer to what his grandmother would have quite accurately called hot and bothered.

He couldn't remember the last time he'd met someone as interesting, smart, funny, and easy on the eyes as Duncan. Add in the strong hits on Joel's gaydar, and he got an irresistible combination not too terribly common in a small town, in Illinois or anywhere else.

The late afternoon sun brought out the warm highlights in Duncan's lovely brown eyes in a way that should have been illegal before nightfall.

Joel's cheeks and ribs got in on the torment with a pleasant ache from smiling and laughing so much, which worked as an unfair partnership for the warmth catapulting through his belly like heat lightning on a summer night.

Duncan chose that moment to sit back on his heels, stretching with his hands over his head. A groan and the line of smooth, dark skin that peeked out from under his silk shirt almost put Joel in a coma.

"That's got a handle on it." Duncan tucked his shirt back

in, glancing at Joel with a shy smile. "Maybe tomorrow we can sort out the ones that are hopelessly outdated, too common, or just plain forgettable. The more we narrow things down, the easier your job gets."

"*Our* job," Joel said, wondering if he was getting ahead of himself. "One of the tricks, at least around here, is coming up with more than one design for Ms. Vincent to choose from. She almost always chooses the one I think she will, but she still insists on at least three options. Maybe you can do one of them, for the practice."

Duncan stared down at his hands, and a weird sinking sensation tugged at Joel's insides.

No sign of a wedding ring, and Duncan hadn't mentioned someone else in his life. Not that he was required to, certainly not on his first day. The omission would be beyond strange as much as they'd already chattered to each other, and about themselves, but not sinister.

Somehow Joel felt like he'd smashed face-first into a prickly wall of secrecy anyway.

"I'm not that great at the design side, Joel. Barely a beginner to tell you the truth. I took this job mainly to get a break from my main gig, you know? And I thought it would be fun, and wow, that part's already the best surprise I've had all *year*."

He looked up at Joel with a hesitant smile, only for an extremely hot second, then busied himself lining up the already neat stacks on the carpet between them.

Joel chewed the insides of his cheeks to keep from lighting up with a dopey grin that would have barely covered the fireworks taking over his chest. Even though the grin would have been an entirely truthful reaction, someone who managed to speak up that much and look so shy while doing it probably wasn't ready for a full-on *hell yes* response.

If the near-instant attraction was mutual, hopefully the weeks before their flashing, neon-red mid-October deadline would give them both time to figure things out.

"That's nothing to feel bad about, Duncan. It's not like you lied on your resume or something like that. And I hope you're not feeling blindsided about what I need you do too."

Duncan looked up and raised one eyebrow.

"Kind of like you being asked to design a physical object like a float folks will ride on without talking to the people who'll actually have to build the thing? Getting dragged into low-key structural design instead of graphic design? No, I don't feel like that at all."

Joel returned Duncan's smile.

"Good. As far as what I needed, what you've already done in getting this tidal wave of paper organized goes well above and beyond. Pretty much anything else will be a fantastic bonus."

Unlike the almost nonstop giggles and laughs since Duncan had walked through the door, the breathy chuckle that escaped him left Joel decidedly uneasy.

"I appreciate that," Duncan said, again staring at the newly contained stacks of paper on the floor. "I'll do my best to help. As far as all these piles, would people get upset if we return the most obvious rejects? Or would it be better to keep them here until you're ready to unveil your final brilliant design?"

Joel did his best to pretend he felt as happy and light as he had all afternoon, though the air between them had turned cool and clammy.

"They take up a lot less space now, so I'd say put those off to the side. That way I won't spend the next couple of months fending off folks who are absolutely convinced if I only saw their ideas one more time, I'd change my mind."

Duncan finally glanced up and smiled, so Joel decided to ignore how troubled those big brown eyes were.

"Makes sense to me. Just show me where to stash those, and we'll get started on the rest."

6

Duncan knew better when he left his apartment the next morning, but he still ended up getting to the Grateful Grocer office a good hour too early.

Long before Joel would arrive, for one thing. And too long before Duncan would have access to that dynamite coffee bomb, which he very much needed today.

Trying to sleep in a place he wasn't used to didn't come close to explaining his dismal night, or the brain fog and headache he'd earned for his pitiful efforts at keeping his eyes closed for more than ten minutes at a time.

A kind soul—a Midwest-friendly and probably more-attentive-than-he-seemed security guard—had taken pity on him instead of leaving him leaning against the building's properly small-town red brick wall.

Or possibly retreating to his car for a nap.

So now he sat quietly in the extra chair Joel had brought in for him yesterday. Staring at the orderly stacks that had replaced the absolute chaos of Joel's little corner of the office.

Not a sound in the rest of the building, and not a sign of another person once the sympathetic security guard had escorted him back here and departed.

Duncan didn't smell even inferior coffee brewing. Only the stale overnight air with a lingering lemon fragrance of some kind of cleaner. Certainly a Grateful Grocer special item.

A golden opportunity to do what he was best at, in other words.

Wander around. Perhaps check in a file cabinet or two. At least glance at the neat desks he'd walked by on his way in yesterday.

Maybe figure out more about why Bonnie Vincent had set him so on edge the day before. It wouldn't be the first time he'd arrived on a job to investigate one thing, but ended up digging into something much more interesting instead.

Duncan leaned back in his chair, staring up at the speckly pattern on the tasteful cream-colored tile ceiling.

The problem was his taste for this gig had pretty much deserted him during the endless, uncomfortable night.

But that wasn't true, not really. He'd lost his feel for the whole thing when Joel offered him the chance to create one of the designs for the damn parade float himself. Basically handing him the opportunity to not only steal the design right up front, but to influence the whole project, at least a little bit.

Reporting back to his *interested party* so early—and taking his chance to sabotage the GG float from within—would no doubt net Duncan a sweet bonus.

But for the first time in all the years of his not-quite-dirty-but-nowhere-near-clean line of work, he couldn't stand the thought of actually doing what he'd been hired for.

All he could see was the awful, betrayed look in Joel's blue eyes when he found out. Odds were astronomically high he'd know exactly who slipped the word to the competitor, too.

New guy, the one who'd shown up out of nowhere? Asking all kinds of questions? Flirting shamelessly?

Duncan spun his chair in lazy circles, letting his eyes drift over Joel's desk, the darkened monitors, the broad window showing a small-town street coming to life.

Flirting on the job wasn't anything new to him, with men or women. That had been one of his best ways to disarm the target, get them to relax and trust him.

His success hadn't bothered him, not once.

Until now.

On his next spin, he realized he was no longer alone.

Joel stood there, handsome and hotter than the day before.

Duncan put his foot down to stop the chair's motion, but his belly and heart continued to swirl in a slow groove at how glad Joel seemed to see him.

Might be Duncan's sleep-deprived imagination, or wishful thinking. Or maybe Joel playing some kind of game of his own.

But damn if seeing that big, warm smile so early in the morning didn't feel amazing.

"Sorry to intrude before you got here," Duncan said. "I

showed up early and a guard let me in. Quite friendly, but I got the feeling he was keeping a close eye on me anyway. I was afraid if I went to the break room unsupervised, I might uncover some other top-secret product."

Joel shook his head and walked toward his desk, now grinning.

"That would be Henry, the building and maintenance supervisor, but you could say he guards the place. He's been here since before Grateful Grocer moved into this building. I have no idea how long. My guess is he understands more about how any company that's been here runs than most of the employees ever will. He gets lists of everyone who's supposed to be onsite every day and somehow never forgets a single face."

"Oh. I thought maybe he just trusted me *on site,* instead of just *on sight.*" Duncan groaned and rubbed his face. "I'm sorry, that was awful. I didn't get much sleep last night."

Joel tucked his green backpack under his desk and leaned against it, staring at Duncan.

"That stinks. Too many Coffee Bombs yesterday?"

Duncan shrugged and got up, trying to hide a yawn behind his hand.

"I doubt it. I'm pretty much a sieve when it comes to caffeine. Probably more like getting used to a new job, new apartment. Too much excitement."

His belly switched to loop-de-loops when Joel blushed, but didn't look away.

"Yeah, I had kind of a restless night myself. Want to hit the break room now that I'm here to keep an eye on you?"

Duncan laughed, hoping it didn't sound too giddy.

That was the other thing that chased him around inside his own head all night long. How much he *liked* Joel, and wanted to be liked back. Not exactly professional for his profession, to say the least.

And pretending he didn't feel that way, letting the emotions sneak around and get ahead of his logic, seemed like a guaranteed path to getting himself into some kind of trouble.

"That's the best idea I've heard all day. We weeded out a lot yesterday, but there's more than enough to dig into that we'll need plenty of brain fuel."

Duncan followed, doing his best not to look too closely at how Joel's forest-green pants emphasized all the right parts when he walked. Better to concentrate on today's golf shirt featuring a subtle, repeating pattern of stylized dinosaurs.

"Where do you get those fabulous nerdy shirts? The best kind of nerdy, I mean. They'd fit in anywhere, but only a fellow brainiac would catch on."

Joel glanced back with a half-smile.

"I stumbled across a shop on a trip to Chicago right after college, with graduation money hot in my pocket. They were having a going out of business sale and I pretty much bought everything they had in my size. You'll be here a while before my geeky fashion show repeats."

This time Duncan hoped his smile didn't look too sickly and guilty. In his experience—leading him ever closer to burnout over the last couple of years—he never stayed anywhere for long. Much less a while.

No matter how much he might want to.

He wanted to talk about Chicago even less, since he'd taken this small-town escape *from* there. Leaving his job, friends, and apartment behind in the process.

He was still trying to think up some other topic to discuss besides his background or Joel's clothing when they rounded the corner into the break room.

And almost crashed headlong into Bonnie Vincent.

"Want to be careful this early in the morning, boys!" she exclaimed in her unnaturally excited voice. "Never know who you might run into when everyone's caffeine and resistance levels are low."

Her manic grin couldn't manage to cover for the cringeworthy attempt at a joke, though Joel only brushed it off with an entirely fake laugh and a wave of one hand.

"Sorry about charging in here like that, Ms. Vincent. We weren't expecting anyone else to be here so early."

Duncan didn't attempt to add a comment of his own. He was too busy taking a closer look at the Grateful Grocer boss than he'd bothered with the day before. When he'd thought his focus would be on a simple spy game of get in, get the secret, and get out.

She still wore the standard-issue high-end golf attire, today with light blue pants and an eye-rending yellow shirt. But now that he'd activated his data-gathering brain in her direction, he noticed a hell of a lot more.

That chopped hairdo might be a 1990s-era chunky blonde-and-brown dye job, but the smooth gloss showed every sign of being expensive, and recently touched up. No wedding ring, but larger diamond stud earrings than would make sense on the golf links or in any business-casual workplace.

She'd slipped up in her total one-sport appearance with a glittering diamond tennis bracelet too, one that was far too big and flashy to be anything but real.

Duncan would have bet the cash he had coming for this gig at least ten times over that Bonnie drove a car that landed far outside the typical expense profile for someone her age in such a small town. He'd done enough quick research into GG over the last week to know the chain didn't bring in that kind of compensation for the CEO.

Or it shouldn't.

She eyed him for a quick, uncomfortably intense second before she focused her scary enthusiasm back on Joel.

"I figure we have to be all hands on deck all the time at *this* time of year, Joel. Too much going on to miss all the excitement. Working on a few huge contracts that should be ready to announce in time for the big parade. I'm sure you'll be able to modify your fantastic design to accommodate a new sponsored deal or three, right?"

Duncan couldn't for the life of him figure out how Joel managed to smile and nod without turning any shade of sickly green.

"Sure thing, Ms. Vincent. Especially with Duncan here to help with all the quick changes."

Duncan cocked his hand in a smartass one-finger salute, not using the finger he wanted to right that moment.

"That is what I'm here for," he said. "I couldn't help learning from someone as great as his job at Joel."

Joel glanced over with a quick smile, and every bit of Duncan's insides spiked up hotter than the coffee he needed more than ever.

Bonnie raised her perfectly shaped eyebrows and smiled, showing more than the necessary amount of perfectly capped and overly white teeth.

"Well, well, well. Sounds like the two of you might turn out to be a great match. Great addition to the GG team, too. Let me get out of your way and leave you to hatch that brilliant design. We're all counting on you."

She brandished a beer-sized blue mug sporting the Grateful Grocer logo toward them and strode out of the room.

Joel shook his head slowly, eyes aimed toward his unbelievably cute green loafers.

"I'm beginning to think she's an acquired taste," he said. "One I haven't quite figured out the right mixer for."

Duncan only managed to keep from snorting out laughter with an extremely stern mini-lecture that made it from his tired brain to his giggle-producing chest just in time.

"This is absolutely none of my business, especially since I just walked in the door yesterday. And I should keep my mouth clamped shut after a rotten night, but apparently I won't. How does *anyone* ever acquire that taste?"

Joel didn't keep nearly as firm a grip on his guffaw as Duncan had, though he smacked one hand over his mouth after the exuberant noise was already out and dancing around the break room.

"I think ingesting a good dose of the top-secret brain fuel

has to be the key, don't you? Looks like Kaylie's either out or has a later shift, which always means she left a stack of butter and sugar goodness tucked away for us somewhere. Between those two, it's got to be a great way to start."

7

Joel's earlier unease about Duncan vanished before he finished tracking down the treats Kaylie had indeed left in the breakfast refrigerator.

Partly because Duncan took it upon himself to seek out cinnamon and ginger Coffee Bombs from one of the cabinets and line four of them up on the counter. The sparkling ribbons of deep red and gold made them almost too pretty to dunk into hot water.

Almost.

Joel busied himself cranking up the miniature convection oven to heat muffin-shaped eggy delights full of onion, red peppers, and plenty of extra-sharp cheddar cheese, one of his favorite grab-and-go offerings from Grateful Grocer.

Adding thick breakfast cookies bursting with walnuts, apple, and brown sugar to the toaster might have seemed like overkill on an ordinary day, or even with all the excitement of the day before.

But Ms. Vincent's near ambush had thrown him off his usual coffee-and-go-morning game.

Not to mention the way Duncan couldn't have been joking about his rough night.

He still looked plenty handsome—especially with today's indigo button-up shirt and curve-hugging black pants. Even Joel couldn't pretend not to see the bloodshot eyes, though, or the slight puffiness underneath.

When he turned away from the oven and its rising aroma of heavenly delights, Duncan had already put out two of the huge mugs Ms. Vincent used. The steam rising from both curled and beckoned to invite him to the table nearest the wall of green plants, only now showing bits of sunlight through their glossy leaves.

He'd be a fool to resist such an enticing display of impending alertness. Especially with Duncan leaning over one of the mugs, breathing in the caffeine molecules before they could escape into the air.

"Got food going to help absorb all that coffee," Joel said. "Hopefully that will balance us out instead of giving us a solid case of the jitters."

Duncan looked toward the convection oven, and his smile handled most of the job of settling Joel's nerves.

"I thought I was the only one teetering on the edge of madness today. Or at least giddiness. I assumed you'd want hot coffee since we're still in the cruel cool-weather phase of the morning, hope that's okay."

"That's what I would have gotten for myself. Not so much because of the weather. More for... I don't know. Comfort, maybe? Kind of like hot chocolate after a rough day at school."

Duncan's solemn, verging on sad expression sent Joel sinking in a dreadful, clenching certainty that he'd ruined everything by being so honest. And sounding like a pouty little boy on top of everything else.

Never mind that he sometimes felt like a kid a breath away from a temper tantrum after an unexpected encounter with Ms. Vincent.

Letting someone else know that was no way to build a good work relationship with his new assistant, much less a friendship.

Anything else was surely already off the table and best not even daydreamed about.

But Duncan only sighed and nodded slowly, without a trace of condescension or irritation.

"Yeah, that kind of thing sucks bad enough at the end of a work day. Having it smack you in the face first thing—before you get your feet settled—can keep you off-balance all day long."

Joel started to turn at the oven's mellow chime, but Duncan touched his arm.

Joel managed not to jump and shiver at the electric surge of contact, but it took a lot out of him.

The startled expression in Duncan's wide eyes made it clear Joel wasn't the only one who noticed the spark.

"I'll get whatever smells so incredible. Sit. Try your coffee. Let me know if it needs anything."

Once Joel got a sip, he was grateful Duncan couldn't see him for more than his shaking hands. Duncan had drizzled exactly the right amount of honey into the mug, even with the double bomb serving. That simple, thoughtful gesture—and the fact that Duncan must have paid close attention to Joel's habits the day before—had Joel's eyes welling with tears.

A hell of a lot more like that rough-day-little-boy than he wanted to admit.

The bright, cheery ding of the toaster saved him from having to compose himself enough to say thank you.

"Are these cookies for us, too?" Duncan's smile was plain in his voice. "They might smell better than the Danishes did yesterday."

Joel blinked before he turned.

"I figured we'd need enough to soak up your double-shot of coffee, which was exactly the right call. And they're full of oats and grains and all kinds of other healthy stuff."

Duncan set a round GG plate decorated with colorful berries and nuts around the edge in front of him, then added a festive yellow napkin with a knife and fork tucked inside. The savory muffin and sweet cookie fit just right.

"Everything a growing boy needs," Duncan said as he sat. "And everything a rattled man needs too, I hope. For my sake. She gave my nerves a jolt, and not the kind I need." He sipped his coffee, then looked up at Joel. "Tell me if I'm way too nosy here, but what's the deal with her? She seems even more... keyed up today."

Joel let out a breath that was just short of a laugh.

"That's an extremely polite—and smart—way to put it. I

haven't been here long enough to hear much of the really juicy gossip, and I'm kind of on my own over in my introvert's office anyway. Not that graphics people seem to mix much, at least in my freelancing experience. So I'm not sure what the real story might be. But she strikes me as on the over-the-top side. I don't think it's drugs, though."

He jumped and grabbed one of the yellow napkins when Duncan almost choked out a mouthful of coffee.

"I'm okay," Duncan managed between coughs. "That just wasn't anything like what I expected you to say. Drugs never crossed my mind. Surprised me is all."

"I don't think it had crossed my mind until just now. But I remember a few kids in college who were speeding on one thing or another, and they kind of acted like that. With her it seems more... This is awful to say, and I hope there aren't any of the wrong kinds of bugs in these plants. But it seems more like an act. A put-on for some reason."

Duncan nodded, eyes still watering and cheeks flushed under his dark skin.

"Makes sense. The behavior, I mean. Seems contrived to me. I don't know why the heck someone would do that, either."

Joel sliced off a bite of his muffin and chewed, marveling as he always did at how the peppers and onions were as crisp as the outside of the crust was crunchy.

"I think if it was me, I'd have to be worried to act that way. You know, trying to make up for something, maybe. Or distract whoever I was talking to."

Duncan nodded. "That or making someone think I was a

hell of a lot more confident than I was. I *never* do that, of course. I content myself with being the naturally freaked out person I often am."

Joel looked up, not sure whether Duncan was faking or being honest. He was focused on his cookie right then, getting a bite and closing his eyes as he chewed.

An entirely understandable reaction, since the apples and walnuts were every bit as crunchy and good as Joel's muffin.

Joel's imagination hitched a ride on the caffeine train now charging through his veins and wondered about other times Duncan might have that same expression.

He cleared his throat and shook his head.

"You sound like me. But I have to say you hide it a lot better than I do. Anyway, I guess we should finish up here and get back at it. If Ms. Vincent is determined to make me redesign the float a few times, we'll need an original design for her to mess up first."

8

Duncan's apartment was fairly nice when it came to the long line of temporary accommodations he'd had over the years. No lease and no questions usually meant no frills, but he'd gotten lucky in this case.

Instead of a bland beige box nowhere near as fancy as a cheap hotel room, he'd settled into the temporarily vacant dwelling of a friend of the person who'd hired him for the gig.

One of the many perks that weren't keeping him as dedicated to the job as he usually was.

The decor could have come straight out of a sitcom from the same era as Bonnie Vincent's hairdo, full of purposely mismatched fabrics all in neutral shades, with an overabundance of pillows and thrift-shop artwork. But everything was neat and comfortable and homey.

Most importantly, the internet was lightning fast.

Once he arranged the pillow cascade overwhelming an

oversized coffee-brown chair and forest-green ottoman, it made a remarkably cozy work-from-home spot. Especially since every other surface, including the kitchen table, played host to an army of odd vases and jars and such meant to hold flowers.

Preferably wildflowers plucked from every local public-access space judging from the photos all over the stainless-steel refrigerator and highlighted maps pinned to a corkboard on the kitchen wall.

Thank all the powers of good housecleaning and a lengthy absence, the place didn't smell like all those flowers, or the pollen they so vigorously shared with the world this time of year. Otherwise he would have been showing up to work sniffling and red-eyed, which would *not* do when face-to-face with someone as irresistible as Joel.

All he smelled right now was the warm, soothing chamomile and mint of the tea.

Duncan hadn't expected to do much work outside the Grateful Grocer's main offices. Not with an assignment as simple as getting the inside scoop on a parade float as the design took shape.

But something about Bonnie Vincent wouldn't stop gnawing around his edges, above and beyond his growing and entirely unprofessional affection for Joel.

Sipping a mug of GG's excellent stress-relief tea, swaddled in his favorite ancient black-shirt-gone-gray and ratty cutoff denim shorts, Duncan honestly hoped to find nothing more than an extremely thrifty business leader who knew how to make every penny stretch. Made sense for the CEO of a grocery chain that promised to do the same for every customer.

Except...

That wasn't the experience of shopping at *any* of the chain's stores, and certainly not in the sleek and high-tech headquarters.

Nothing about GG was bare bones or discount, or even gave the appearance of being cost-conscious.

Not Whole Foods level of extravagance and expense by any means. But nowhere near small Midwestern chain frugality, either.

It wasn't just the absurd advertising budget and stream of over-the-top ideas for the damn parade float, either. Every store-brand product was as good as the tea, or the coffee bomb, or those breakfast muffins he'd been craving ever since that morning.

The bakery and butcher shop in each store was big-city quality, and the seafood they managed to stock this far away from any ocean boggled the mind.

And still he might have put all of that aside except for Bonnie's odd twitchiness. Her jittery sense of trying so hard to look and act like someone genuinely interested, but over-shooting well into borderline spooky.

So he fired up his own unusually overpowered laptop and started digging, leaving the usual search channels behind after only a few minutes.

Duncan had never succumbed to the lure of government spying, though he considered it from time to time. Usually after one of his clients escalated to demanding the kind of information even an FBI agent would have had a hard time prying loose.

None of that meant he refused to waltz around the line between legal and illegal information gathering, at least as far as the general public understood it.

Getting a private investigator license a few years ago on a whim paid for itself with the tools he had access to these days.

Including background checks and data scoops that would frighten most civilians into doing their best to stay offline forever.

But in the case of Bonnie Vincent, nothing jumped out in her background no matter how much he dug. Nothing except how relentlessly *ordinary* her life seemed to be.

As in mirror-smooth, not a smudge or blemish, *unnaturally* ordinary.

Duncan was examining a woman who might have been copied and pasted out of some kind of manual called *How to Create a Background Character* or *A Guide to Fitting In*. Maybe even *Models for Middle Management* or *MBA Lifestyles*.

Good in school, but not *too* good. Solid college, but nothing flashy. Career started smoothly, then advanced like clockwork. Plenty of social connections, including a string of long-term boyfriends. Married at twenty-five.

Which turned out to be the exact average age of first marriage the year she did it.

Mortgage and everything else paid on time, including the car he'd scoped on the way through the parking lot that afternoon. Her wheels weren't as expensive as he'd expected from the looks of her jewelry and clothing. The house in her name was new, but not a gigantic mansion.

Not a mark on her credit and no criminal record, either.

None of that would have bothered Duncan most of the time, except to make him wonder how in the world someone could go through life without chipping the paint a few times.

The problem was Bonnie hadn't struck him as the tiniest bit average. She wasn't one to live her little life and blend into the background of small-town Midwestern life, or any kind of life he could think of.

Something was off here.

Unless his blooming appreciation for Joel had knocked every last one of his instincts and hard-earned skills offline, Bonnie Vincent's background looked too average to be true because it was.

Someone had either wiped the slate of her life overly clean—to the point of turning her into something more mannequin than human—or the whole identity was a fake.

Either way, that wasn't the kind of cover job that anyone involved with a grocery chain should be able to do. Even an overly successful one.

Tea finished, Duncan set the cup aside and stared at the only thing that marked this apartment as firmly set in the second decade of the new millennium rather than the end of the last one.

A gigantic flat-screen television that reflected him tucked into his chair as clearly as the perfect mirror of Bonnie Vincent's life.

His reflection shook its head, and Duncan had to agree.

This was *not* his assignment, nor what was going to get him paid. It was most definitely not any kind of way to take a break and clear his head after his brush with near-burnout.

And yet he knew deep in his own rather smudged and flawed and cracked self that he wasn't going to be able to stop at ferreting out some ridiculous parade float design.

Not that he imagined Joel would design anything ridiculous.

Duncan wasn't even sure he was willing to carry through with the original gig now. For more reasons than his developing crush.

He might have stumbled into a case a hell of a lot more interesting, and possibly far-reaching, than he'd had for a while.

Trying to ignore the tingle of excitement pinballing through his brain right now was a waste of time, no matter how much he might want to. This was exactly the kind of promise of discovery that got him into the spy game to begin with.

He grinned at his television-bound self, then shut down his laptop. Time for his mid-assignment ritual of a hot bath and early curling up in bed for a couple of hours with a good book. The nice adventure science fiction novel about as thick as his grandfather's Large Print Bible he'd brought with him would do nicely.

Nothing else that didn't involve more-than-healthy amounts of booze or a friendly bout of casual, no-strings-attached sex would work now that he'd glimpsed the flash of a puzzle to solve.

Even if it wasn't the one he was supposed to be solving.

Every time he'd followed his leads in unexpected directions, it had been well worth the detour in the end.

As he headed toward the neutral-toned bedroom and another round of get all the damn pillows out of the way, he allowed himself the indulgence of imagining Joel waiting for him.

Sex with Joel wasn't likely to be casual, and Duncan couldn't help hoping it wouldn't be no-strings-attached.

If it ever happened.

The trouble was if Joel ever learned the truth about Duncan—that his confessed background was almost as fake as Bonnie's—there would be no chance in hell of friendship between them, much less anything more.

Duncan hoped it wouldn't come to that.

But he couldn't imagine any way to avoid it in the end.

9

Duncan's quiet, distant mood started Joel's day off worried, no matter how many times Duncan swore nothing was wrong.

It wasn't like Joel hadn't stayed up too late reading about a thousand times himself. The last time a few weeks ago, before the Great Parade Float Design Emergency had taken over his entire life.

But he still couldn't shake his uneasiness at the change in Duncan's demeanor.

Or his own queasy suspicion that he'd somehow caused it.

The one positive outcome of nowhere near their usual level of discussion of everything under the sun was all the design suggestions were finally wrangled to a manageable pile. And Duncan had even helped sort what was left into little themed stacks.

Enough so Joel actually had a glimmer of how he might come up with three coherent proposals over the next day or so.

Plenty of time for Ms. Vincent to shoot every one of them down. Or possibly worse, insist on changes that made them all unusable.

They'd just finished pinning the useful images to three huge corkboards so Joel could sketch out his starting points when Duncan spoke about something besides work for the first time all day.

"What do you do for fun around here? After the overwhelming excitement of work, I mean."

Joel shrugged, not wanting to charge forward and seem too eager.

"They have night swims out at the county pool, sometimes with movies on a big inflatable screen. I think this week is summer horror."

"No, I meant what do *you* do," Duncan said.

Joel looked up, surprised to see an oddly determined smile on Duncan's face.

"You mean besides obsess over this place and study design trends until I fall asleep?"

"Yeah, that part I think you've got the hang of. So do I. I'm thinking about something else, and some*where* else."

Joel opened his mouth, but a goofy laugh escaped before any words did.

"I can't believe I'm about to admit this, but I wasn't kidding about what I do. Since I started this job, anyway. Pathetic as it sounds, Grateful Grocer really has taken over my life."

Duncan raised his eyebrows and leaned forward, hands on his knees.

"In that case, you need me for a hell of a lot more than this float insanity. I haven't been here long, but it's too long for me not to know anything besides my apartment and this office. It's Friday. I need someone to clue me in on the best ways to blow off steam."

Joel decided to pretend his cheeks weren't as red as they were hot. His imagination had darted off in entirely not-safe-for-work directions.

"Well, besides the night swims, there's a big batting cage complex outside of town."

"Batting cage?" Duncan grinned. "You mean *baseball* batting?"

"I do mean baseball batting, though I have to wonder what other kind you were thinking about. It serves all the small towns out here. Some kind of tax deal for the county, I think. There are practice fields out there too, and a bunch of those rebounding nets so you can practice fielding. And of course, GG is a major donor for the whole facility."

"Does that mean we get free admission?"

Joel couldn't help grinning back. Despite being quiet and withdrawn all day long, now Duncan sounded and looked like a little kid itching to get outside and onto the playground.

"Free admission, and free food and drinks, too. I just have to flash my employee badge and we're in. I've been meaning to go since it got warm. Just haven't made the time."

He didn't add that he hadn't met anyone he'd want to do such a thing with since he'd started the job, either.

Duncan sat back and rubbed his hands together.

"I haven't swung a bat in ages. Never was all that great at it, but I always loved to try. I can feel the blisters starting already. So, you in?"

Joel glanced at the clock, then down at the preliminary sketches he'd made with his tablet. Rough, sure, and in need of a heck of a lot more detail.

But he had that warm, solid feeling in his chest he got when he started something that was going to turn out good.

No matter what Ms. Vincent thought.

And damned if he hadn't earned a bit of relaxation over the last few months.

"Okay, I'm in. I did my best with baseball, especially with my uncle as the coach, but I was more comfortable as a soccer player growing up. So you have to promise not to laugh at how bad I might be at it after all this time."

Duncan laughed, then covered his mouth with one hand.

"I'm sorry, that's not at you. Like I said, I wasn't exactly an All Star. I don't think I'll get hit, but I have managed to get hit in a batting cage before. In the outfield, too. And when I tried to play soccer, I kicked the ground so hard I had bruised toes for a week. We'll have to promise not to laugh at each other. Deal?"

Joel held out one hand.

"Deal."

The contact between them hit like lightning.

Rippling, long-lasting, summer-night heat lightning.

The kind that circled and promised and threatened all

night long, but never built up enough force to turn destructive.

Every inch of Joel's skin tingled and the hair on his arms stood on end.

From the way Duncan caught his breath, the sensation was mutual.

"So we'll have to..." Joel stopped and cleared his throat. "I mean, I guess we need to go home and change clothes, right? These loafers aren't the best choice for the batting box."

Duncan blinked and shook his head.

"Yeah, I think that's a good idea. Sneakers, I guess? I don't have any of those special shoes with spikes on the bottom."

"And t-shirts, and jeans," Joel said. "Or shorts, since it's gonna still be hot out there. Hot enough for swimming, so whatever's cool."

Duncan's eyes lit up again.

"Should I bring swim trunks too? What's the movie tonight? Did you say something about summer horror?"

Joel took the excuse to break the magnetic eye contact and turn to his computer.

What the hell was going on here? He'd had his share of quick attractions, and acted on them, but nothing that sizzled him head to toe like this.

No one had ever cared about workplace romance when he was a contractor, and he hadn't been at GG long enough to find out if there was a specific policy against it.

But most of him didn't give a damn about things like that right now, with that heat still dancing through him inside and out.

He saved and closed his sketches and ran a quick search.

"Looks like they're showing *Midsommar* tonight. I heard that one's great if you're up for folk horror. Doesn't start until nine, so we'd have plenty of time to see how bad we both are at baseball first. What do you think?"

Joel looked at Duncan in time to see his shoulders slowly rise and fall, and to catch what was surely a lust-addled expression on his handsome face.

He wasn't sure whether he *hoped* it was lust or not.

"I think we'd be insane to miss seeing that movie under the stars," Duncan said. "And I think this project gives us plenty of reason to let off steam by hitting little white balls as hard as we can. Assuming we can hit them at all."

That got an overly loud snort of laughter out of Joel, and the shared giggling fit let a little of the charge out of the air between them.

But nowhere near all of it.

"Let's get out of here before someone decides we're having too much fun," Joel said. "Otherwise we might get sentenced to build the float all by ourselves when the time comes."

10

By the time he went home, changed clothes, and made it to what looked like a gigantic chainlink-and-net big-top circus tent dropped in the middle of a soybean field, Duncan hadn't made much progress in figuring out what had possessed him.

Not that scorching hot handshake with Joel. The origins of his whole-body reaction weren't hard to figure out at all, even if the timing was seriously unexpected.

Not what made him think he could possibly manage to avoid making an utter fool of himself at the batting cage, either. He'd done his fair share of athletics growing up. More of the tennis and track and field variety than baseball, so he should at least be able to keep hold of the bat.

Maybe.

But he still had no clue what made him ask Joel about fun

things to do, much less basically insist Joel do something with him.

He stepped out of the car and into a sensory feast a thousand times removed from his cold-weather memories of mostly indoor or clay tennis courts and chilly spring tracks.

The grass on the practice fields must have just been mown that day to smell so fresh and sharply green. A chorus of woody *thunks* and metallic *pings* from the arrangement of black nets in the middle of the complex had to come from the batting cages.

He hadn't considered needing something to cover the top, but with a ring of practice fields the netting overhead only made sense. He could too easily imagine himself getting hit right on top of the head by someone else's popup while desperately trying to catch a ground ball.

Especially when he'd ranged far outside his goal in spending time with Joel in the first place. He'd be damned if they talked about that blasted parade float or anything else work-related tonight. He wasn't getting paid by the hour for the spy gig anyway.

A long building to the right—painted in Grateful Grocer colors, since he couldn't escape them—advertised itself as the source of both admissions and concessions.

Hopefully the included gift shop would have some kind of gloves to keep his hands from ending up with what he assumed would be a mass of painful blisters.

And surely they had helmets, right?

Still, with his nerves getting away with him before he'd even seen Joel, Duncan loved the feel of the warm late afternoon breeze. The sounds of kids and grownups laughing as they darted around the practice fields.

The prospect of doing something physical and (hopefully) fun, then an evening of lounging in cool water.

All those daydreaming thoughts drifted away like dandelion fluff that would never be allowed near those emerald-green outfields when a transformed Joel strolled toward him.

Not a trace of the anxious, borderline-desperate guy who worked too damn hard at GG, and not quite one of the arrogant jocks Duncan had avoided when he could in high school. Even when he thought they were unreasonably attractive.

Joel managed to create an even more appealing hybrid. Starting with the rock-solid confidence of his walk, all fluid, easy movement rather than his tense, quick stride at work.

Cute and clever as his stealth-nerd day job shirts were, the soft, well-worn gray t-shirt fit like it had been tailor-made for him. The way the blue baseball cap pulled down over his hair brought out the vivid color of his eyes was downright unfair.

But not nearly as unfair as his *legs*.

A perfectly respectable pair of old-school black cargo shorts revealed Duncan's favorite combination of muscular calves and thighs outlined with a luxurious amount of reddish blond hair.

If Joel ever wore shorts to work, Duncan wouldn't get a damn thing done besides staring.

On the other hand, keeping any body part that damn fine under cover should be illegal somewhere.

That freedom of flesh might explain the loose, almost

sensual way Joel moved. Either the clothes or the setting itself freed him up in some way that was flat-out irresistible.

The only thing that got Duncan's mind working again was realizing he didn't look at all out of place in his own green t-shirt and better-kept denim shorts than the ones he lounged around in.

Joel wasn't creepy or obvious about it, but his slow head-to-toe appraisal made it clear Duncan didn't look half bad himself.

They'd both better keep their sensible brains about them this evening.

Duncan couldn't say for sure from Joel's side, but he didn't pretend temptation hadn't already gotten way too far inside his own imagination.

"Quite a setup they've got here," Duncan said, forcing himself to look around so he wouldn't fixate on Joel's legs. "I think I'd get lost if I didn't have a capable guide."

Joel's disarming grin wiped out a good portion of the sensible brain Duncan was depending on.

"Then we're both in trouble," Joel said, "since I've never been out here before. Kids' teams seem to do just fine, so I think we'll be okay if we watch each other's backs."

Duncan coughed back a laugh, because the increasingly useless lump in his skull insisted Joel meant watch each other's back*sides*, which was no help whatsoever.

"Maybe they have a map for beginners," Duncan said. "Or something like those little training wheels for bicycles. They have side blades for ice skates now. I could have used those when I was learning."

Joel raised one eyebrow.

"You're way ahead of me there. I barely managed to keep myself from falling long enough to make it around the rink once or twice. Thank goodness we're not paying for our possible humiliation."

They made it to the building, weaving through a crowd of mostly kids with enough frazzled-looking adults in tow to keep things orderly. To Duncan's great relief, the cheerful teenaged attendant inside supplied him with a scuffed but serviceable red helmet to go with a pair of almost-new white leather gloves.

Joel gave himself another dose of fabulous guy points by producing a burgundy baseball cap from his back pocket.

"It's old, but it's clean. Something to put between your head and the helmet."

Duncan wished he had a mirror to make sure he didn't look ridiculous, but Joel's approving smile would have to be enough.

His anxiety kicked in again when faced with a dizzying array of bats.

"I don't even know whether to pick wood or aluminum," he said, fussing with his gloves.

"Well, we're not in Little League or playing in college. So wood it is." Joel stepped back and looked Duncan up and down again, but in a far more clinical than sensual way. Then he grabbed a bat and handed it over. "We're about the same height, but you're lighter. Give this one a try."

The pale brown wooden handle seemed too thin, like the barrel end would snap off if Duncan managed to make contact with anything. Joel picked up a bat for himself and held it with both hands almost at the flared end.

Duncan shifted his hands down and his grip felt more solid at once.

"All right, I'm ready to hit something. Hopefully not myself."

Joel flipped his own bat up to his shoulder, then touched Duncan's arm. The electric charge didn't hit quite as hard as it had with their hands, but Duncan couldn't pretend it wasn't there.

And the truth was he didn't want to.

"That's what the helmet's for," Joel said. "Come on, those kids left a bunch of open spots. I wouldn't be surprised if a bunch of my co-workers were here too after the last few weeks. We better grab a cage."

Duncan smiled, but the tension between the two parts of himself only got tighter.

He liked Joel *way* too much to betray him by spying on his design, right?

And ratting out what he was more certain by the minute was a juicy, perhaps illegal secret keeping Grateful Grocer on such flashy financial footing wouldn't likely endear him to Joel or anyone else in town.

The worst part was Duncan knew which side of himself was likely to win out in the end.

The same side that had kept him great at his job, and alone and lonely way too damn much already.

11

It was everything Joel could do to keep from sprinting toward two empty spots along the rounded line of batter's boxes.

Each rectangle of brown rubberized surface held its own home plate, with plenty of room on each side for lefties or righties to step in and get comfortable. One end of the cage-like box was open to a central hub full of machines with no other purpose but hurling baseballs or softballs at high speed toward humans who paid for the privilege.

Right now, only a few of the cages were occupied, with men and women swinging hard enough to grunt every time a ball *thooped* toward them. All of them were well past their Little League days, so odds were high stress relief came along with every solid contact.

A few ground balls jumped and skittered back to the central area, but most got launched, with several only stopping once they hit the high fenced backstop or the black net overhead.

With every step, Joel switched between wanting to make sure he'd be beside Duncan, and wondering if they might be better off with a lot more space between them than a chain link fence.

Before he could make up his whirling mind, Duncan spoke from behind him.

"Those two might be best. On the end there. So I won't look too bad."

Joel turned back and rolled his eyes.

"You look great, and I expect you'll do just fine."

He faced forward again in time to squeeze his face into an amused scowl, wondering what his runaway mouth thought it was playing at. That was way more truth than he'd planned to let out into the soft summer afternoon air just then.

Duncan's laugh set what felt like a thousand fly balls dancing around in Joel's belly.

"Well, if one person who knows what he's doing has that much confidence in me, I'll give it a go."

Joel pulled open the fence door on the cage at the end of the row, set beside a black rubber backstop that went from the ground to about chest-high.

"You take this one, and helmet on before you step in there. The pitching machine won't go until we start it, but it's a good habit to get into. Or do you want to watch me try for a few first? I doubt very much I have any kind of a textbook swing, but I've got the general idea."

Duncan closed his eyes for a second and nodded.

"Yes, please. I don't even know how to get it started. And my real worry is I don't know how to get it to *stop*."

Joel moved to the next cage over and stepped inside. He held up a card kind of like a hotel room key, then gave one to Duncan as he waved him to follow.

"This place is absurdly high-tech compared to what was around when we were kids. More than batting cages pretty much anywhere else from what I hear, but it's easier than juggling a bunch of quarters. Most people pay for a certain amount of time, and employees usually reserve a block as long as they're not too crowded. It's slow right now, so we can stay as long as we want."

He put his own helmet on, thankful it didn't stink of sweat from whoever used it last. Whatever the staff sprayed them with in between had a strong enough fresh pine aroma to cover it up. Even with his own cap firmly in place, he decided to believe the attendant's claim that no one had ever caught anything from them, either.

Duncan wrinkled his nose, smiled, and put his on.

"Don't feel like you have to swing away," Joel said. "Especially since we're not paying by the pitch. Just keep your bat on your shoulder and watch a few go by. Let yourself get a feel for how long it takes for the ball to get to the backstop."

Joel slid his card into a metal slot set into the fence beside the door, very much aware of how closely Duncan watched his every move. That brown-eyed gaze felt like heat against his skin.

"Most of the time you have to get in the cage set to the speed you want to swing at. But these machines are adjustable." He tapped the white-on-green box in the blocky display with "50 MPH" in the middle.

"Oh thank goodness," Duncan said, pretending to brace himself against the chain wall. "I was terrified you were going to pick eighty or ninety."

"Not likely! I might work up to sixty, maybe, but this is plenty fast to start with. I'd hate to conclude my demonstration by getting knocked out by a machine and forcing you to rescue me."

Something in Duncan's eyes made Joel acutely aware of just how small the batting cage was, even though there was plenty of room for one. With two—and the mind-of-its-own attraction growing between them—the space felt like an old-school phone booth with the door closed.

"Okay, well, for this part, it's better if you watch."

Duncan nodded, then let out an embarrassed laugh and grinned.

"Oh, you mean from *outside*, right? Of course you do. I'm such a dork. That would be the best possible scenario, wouldn't it? Both of us knocked out cold while it keeps pitching and pitching and pitching."

He darted outside and clanked the door closed, still laughing under his breath.

"No worries," Joel said. "I wasn't exactly clear. You can watch from there or from your side. I'm going for it. And again, no laughing if I swing and miss hard enough to twist myself into the ground."

Duncan took another of those somehow suggestive deep breaths.

"No laughing. I promise."

Joel held Duncan's intense gaze as long as he could stand it before focusing on the little display again.

"All that's left now is pushing *Start* and getting into the batter's box when you're ready. Or watching a few."

He tapped the correct spot on the screen and stepped to the outside of the white rectangle on the ground, gripping the bat hard, hoping that hid his shaking hands.

A light on the metal-framed machine just over sixty feet away blinked red three times, then the light shone green.

A baseball *thooped* toward him and thunked off the rubber backstop, rattling the chain-link.

"No wonder you said to watch," Duncan said. "No way I can even *see* that."

"It looks a little different from in here. And we can always set it a little slower until you get comfortable." Joel let one more go by, judging the speed and angle before he moved closer to home plate, bat on his right shoulder. "Let's see what happens."

When the light flashed green again, he sank into the stance he hadn't taken for almost ten years.

His thinking mind slipped away.

He started his swing before the ball even left the machine's grip.

And made solid contact, sending a good grounder skittering away. His hands and shoulders thrummed.

"Great one, Joel!"

Joel nodded, but the next pitch was already on the way.

This time his timing was closer, and the line drive flew straight back toward the machine.

"That one felt better," he said. "I was off on the first. Let me try…"

He shifted his hands and swung, sending the next one soaring into the overhead net."

"Wow," Duncan said. "You're better than you let on."

Joel laughed, still focused on the machine's warning lights.

"What is it people say?" He got under the next one, and it launched almost straight up. "Like riding a bike?"

"I don't know if I can follow you in there. Not riding a bike, I'm pretty good at that." Duncan paused when Joel smacked another pitch hard toward what would be right field. "You haven't missed one."

"I haven't gotten tired yet. But I will."

Joel hit several more before he stepped backward and jabbed the "Stop" button on the panel, then waited until the machine's lights went dark.

He paused for a second, amazed at his body's exhilarated reaction to something he hadn't enjoyed all that much as a kid. When he'd been more or less forced into it by his overenthusiastic father and an uncle as the coach who wouldn't argue with his own big brother.

Now his whole body tingled, especially his hands. He breathed hard but deep and steady, with his heart beating faster and stronger than it should have from basically standing in one place.

He wanted more than anything to get the tireless mechanical pitcher going again and swing away.

Well, *almost* more than anything.

Because the prospect of watching Duncan move and shift and twist his body sent an entirely different set of tingles into motion.

He turned to see a grinning Duncan standing right behind the backstop, peeking over like a little boy, eyes wide and excited. Figuring out what *kind* of excited would have to wait for later.

Joel grinned back.

"Your turn."

12

For a second, Duncan wasn't sure whether the fear, desire, or guilt would win out inside his thunderstorm head.

Watching Joel do something as calm and ordinary as sorting out an absurd stack of design suggestions, creating new ones on his computer, or even making freaking *coffee* was stimulating enough.

Way more than spending time with someone he intended to steal from should be. That thought sent a sickly bolt of guilt twisting through his gut, threatening to spoil everything else, inside and out.

But watching Joel do something Duncan would have *thought* was ordinary, like hitting a baseball?

Dangerously exciting.

The way those gorgeous legs flexed when he crouched. The ripple of muscles in his arms when he gripped and shifted the bat. The quick, coordinated motion of his whole body when he swung the bat.

Not just his arms and shoulders, though that would have been trouble enough.

Joel started his swing with his dead-sexy legs, and continued with his hips in a most enticing way. The follow-through with his arms and shoulders just turned all that movement up way past eleven.

Still, it was the deep, guttural grunt that was going to leave Duncan with the vapors, as he'd heard one of his grandmothers say.

But when Joel turned to look at Duncan, breathing hard, with an unreasonably sexy flush on that handsome face? And an I-dare-you glint in his gorgeous blue eyes?

It was everything Duncan could do to keep from melting into an overheated puddle on the ground.

Given the tiniest bit of encouragement, he'd take his turn for damn sure. And it wouldn't be at this very fancy batting cage or anywhere else clothing was required.

"But you're doing so *well*, Joel. Won't it be bad luck for me to step in now and break your rhythm?"

Damn. The image his adolescent-kid brain conjured for that wasn't helping matters.

"The way I see it is you wanted to learn, right? I wouldn't be much of a teacher if I didn't give you the opportunity to do that, would I?"

Now Duncan's heart picked up the tempo almost as much as the mess of images rampaging in his mind.

Back at the Grateful Grocer office—under the glaring

lights and with Joel wearing long pants and in his harried designer mode—Duncan might have enjoyed words like that, but he would have added in the flirtatious side in his imagination.

Out here in the late afternoon sun, with sweat beading on Joel's arms, and the bat he knew how to handle way better than he'd let on parked on his shoulder?

With a gaze equal parts direct and electric, focused on Duncan and no way to doubt how many not-at-all-safe-for-work ideas waiting behind it?

Duncan would be a fool to pretend he wasn't firmly in the middle of a hell of a lot more than learning how to hit a baseball.

"I suppose you're right," he said, gripping his bat with a confidence he didn't feel. "I wouldn't be much of a student if I didn't at least try. Your cage or mine?"

"Let's go to yours so you can set everything up yourself."

Duncan was glad of the excuse to look away, and the few steps to the next door in the chain link to catch his breath. He wasn't much more than a breath away from getting in over his head.

Knowing that didn't seem to make much of a difference. Certainly not when Joel followed him into the cozy space of his own batting cage.

Making sure his helmet was secure on his head, Duncan pulled out the little hotel room card. His fluttering stomach sank when he spotted a huge GG ad on one side.

Maybe that reminder of why he was there in the first

place was a good thing, no matter how annoying it felt in the moment.

He put the card into the little metal box and couldn't help smiling when the screen lit up.

"I think forty miles per hour is more my speed."

"Hang on, why don't you get in a few swings first? I should have, but I was too happy to be in a batting cage without someone forcing me to be there. And criticizing my every move."

Joel rolled his eyes and shook his head.

"Never mind all that. Go ahead and step in so I can take a look."

Duncan stood in the little white box, glad he was right-handed like Joel so the stance would be easy to copy. He bent his knees, leaned forward at the waist, and held the bat over his shoulder.

"Feel comfortable?" Joel said. "Balanced, like you can get a good swing?"

"I think so. Step back and I'll try."

Joel moved to the back of the cage, and Duncan once again *felt* his gaze. He wouldn't be surprised if parts of his body lit up red everywhere Joel looked.

The first swing felt awkward and stiff, from his waist up instead of starting with his feet. He didn't have to ask to know he had a long way to go to get to Joel's smooth motion.

"We probably should have warmed up first," Joel said. "That goes double for me because I got plenty of practice at that as a kid. Just relax. This is supposed to be fun."

Duncan laughed, but inside he wondered how unpleasant

Joel's experience playing as a kid had been. And how much he'd hate it when he realized how deceitful Duncan had been since the first second they'd met.

"I take it I looked as awkward as I felt, huh?"

He swung again, and everything moved more easily.

"There you go," Joel said. "Keep your feet solid and drive from there. The most important thing right now is watching for the ball. We can worry about fine-tuning your mechanics later. If you want to. Ready to give it a go?"

"As I'll ever be. You definitely should step out before I do. I'd hate to lose my grip and smack you with the bat."

Joel walked around to the other cage.

"You'll do fine. No one's keeping count. Want me to watch or not?"

Oh, the ideas in Duncan's mind had no place where kids had been running around not even an hour ago.

"Yeah, watch the first few swings, so you can tell me how I do."

Duncan had no problem letting the first few pitches go by, and the sound as they thudded into the backstop was so much louder than he expected. But *sooner* than he expected, he wanted to see what he could do.

Besides looking dangerously powerful and hot, the way Joel's whole body moved as one connected whole when he made contact looked like an absurd amount of fun.

He stepped forward, watching for that light to flash red the third time.

As soon as it did, he breathed out, letting his body relax.

And coiled his energy at the same time.

Seeing the ball go by several times let his eyes know what to look for.

And his swing let loose all by itself.

The glancing contact stung his hands and arms, but the ball did not fly all the way past untouched.

"*Hell* yes," he said under his breath, or thought he did, as it bounced not far in front of him.

"Feels great, doesn't it?"

Duncan laughed again, but he didn't look away from those blinking lights.

"Like I never would have believed."

He sent the next pitch skittering away on a much straighter line.

Then got a good solid hit and sent it on a line back toward the machine.

"Now you've got it," Joel said.

Duncan didn't realize Joel had started his machine again until a second baseball came flying out almost at the same time his own did. That little distraction earned him his first swing and miss.

But since Joel ripped his pitch in a high arc, Duncan decided his miss must have gone unnoticed.

In any case, he was too focused on the next one to worry too much about it.

He had no idea how many times he'd swung when Joel spoke again.

"Ready to take a break?"

Duncan stepped backward, too jolted out of his concentration to be sure he wouldn't get hit.

The second he straightened up, his thighs, lower back, and shoulders finally broke through, in a screamingly loud chorus all about how long overdue a break was.

He shook his head and stepped back again, just as a pitch whizzed by.

"Yeah, I guess I've been at it a while, huh?"

"Just over an hour. Doesn't sound like much, but I get the feeling it was enough. Just hit *Stop* on the display."

Straightening his fingers turned the chorus of complaints up to a screech inside his head. He ended up using a knuckle to shut the machine down before turning to see Joel waiting outside the cage.

"An *hour?* Really?"

Joel nodded, flexing his own fingers, bat leaning against the fence.

"I lost track of the time myself, sorry about that. We're both going to be sore as hell tomorrow."

Sure enough, the sun had tracked a good way toward the horizon, and everyone else who'd been swinging away was gone. A new crowd of what looked like late teenagers were gathering at the other end of the cages.

"I guess I won't know for sure until I wake up," Duncan said, "but right now I'll say it was worth every ache and pain. I haven't gotten that much out of my head with clothes on since—"

He stopped, pretending to cough, and knowing he wasn't fooling anybody.

Joel's grin verified that a second later.

"Me too. Come on, we get free food too. Then we'll be ready for swimming if you still want to."

"Now that I've gotten about a year's worth of frustrations out, swimming sounds like the best possible therapy."

Duncan made it out of the cage without hobbling too badly. But he got plenty of warning from his muscles that cramps would be immediately delivered if he didn't give them a rest, and *now*.

Even less welcome was the sticky clench of guilt in his belly at the way Joel looked at him.

Like a lover would look at him.

Or at least a trusted friend.

Worse, one who trusted him in return.

Maybe he'd balanced in the whirlwind between desire and guilt too long already, a dance he never should have started in the first place. No spy gig—no matter how well it paid—was worth putting Joel or himself through more of this.

Even if Duncan wanted to keep going for his own selfish reasons.

The biggest problem was figuring out how he'd let himself get in so deep, and how he could possibly dig himself out.

13

Joel decided the outdoor seating area was the only possible choice for two guys who'd just spent much longer than they meant to sweating and hitting baseballs over and over again.

Not to mention how much better a private conversation sounded than doing their best to hear each other in the crowd of kids starting to fill the place up.

Instead of the plain wooden picnic tables he remembered from his playing days—often full of splinters, carved obscenities, and artistic uses of spent bubble gum—they found a collection of red and blue tables almost as nice as in GG's break room.

He headed toward one of the small round ones, as far away as possible from the longer models sure to attract the chattering high-schoolers. The addition of a series of huge, overlapping white and blue umbrellas overhead to cut down on some of the lingering heat was a bonus.

The circular setup was a lot like a miniature version of the batting cages, with chain link all around and black netting across the top. All the better to avoid getting knocked in the head by a stray white missile.

Neither the net nor the umbrellas blocked the mouth-watering aroma of grilling and baking coming from inside the building.

Not that he wished Duncan ill, far from it. But Joel took *some* comfort in not being the only one walking a bit awkwardly.

He felt like his own thighs and calves were going to seize up any second, which played especially well with the ache in his lower back. The gloves seemed to have protected his hands well, though his grip on a sweating bottle of water was shaky at best. Joel had never been more grateful to have to wait for someone else to carry his food out.

Only time would tell whether he'd be able to use a mouse or his drawing stylus once Monday rolled around.

Of course if things went the way he hoped with Duncan— and the way the free-roaming excitement heating up his body suspected they would—a lot more might change before Monday than challenges with his hands.

All changes for the better.

He sat with less of a groan than he expected, doing his best to give a sympathetic smile when Duncan grimaced.

"I'm going to regret all of this tomorrow, aren't I?"

Catching what sounded like an honestly regretful tone in Duncan's voice, Joel decided to hold on to the exhilaration and confidence he'd gotten back in touch with, doing something as simple and difficult as hitting a round ball with a straight bat.

"Overdoing it is probably going to hit us both in the muscles, yeah. But I hope you don't regret *all* of it."

Duncan's smile had an uncomfortable edge that didn't fit the situation or the conversation.

"I hope not too," he said. "Sometimes these things just get...off, no matter how much you don't want them to."

Joel shook his head and took a long drink of his cold water. Grateful Grocer's hot-selling store brand, of course, even more crisp and refreshing than usual.

"I'm afraid you lost me there," he said. "That could be because of the heat as much as my brain reacting to watching too many baseballs thrown toward me at high speed."

Duncan stared at the table, then swallowed half of his own water. He pulled the cap Joel had loaned him off, leaving his hair a spiky, sweaty mess.

"Maybe that's what's going on with me. Overextended my brain as much as the rest of me." Duncan's voice wasn't quite convincing, even though the words made sense. "I had a fantastic time batting, Joel. Way more than I thought I would when we decided to do this. To be fair, when I pretty much pushed you into it."

Joel couldn't keep a huge, surely goofy grin off his face. The kind of expression he might have worn if he'd had a hell of a lot more fun playing baseball as a kid instead of what felt like constant stress.

"You were *killing* it toward the end. You've got a great natural eye. We might have to break out the gloves next time and see how you do with throwing and fielding. If you want."

"If you teach me, I bet I'd do just fine. You're as good with that as you are with the design and computers stuff. If you're that good with such a beginner, I'd say you could coach kids or anyone else if you wanted to."

This time Joel shook his head, but the grin stayed put.

He hadn't expected to have such a wonderful time batting himself, but coaching Duncan had turned out to be a delight. In more ways than one.

"I appreciate you saying so, but you really did pick it up fast."

A girl who looked about seventeen brought their food and more water, giving Joel a chance to think about how dead sexy Duncan looked as he got into the groove of hitting.

Finding the sharp focus that let him follow the ball and swing at the right time.

Gradually moving his hips, then his back and shoulders.

Anyone who could get coordinated that fast with something new would likely make a hell of an athlete no matter what they tried.

Probably be great at all kinds of other physical activities, too.

Joel distracted himself by turning toward his food, popping a couple of almost-too-hot fries into his mouth. The cheeseburger really would have to cool a bit to avoid a conversation-challenging scorched tongue.

"Are you a natural swimmer too?" he said. "Not that we'll have to swim much at all tonight."

Duncan grabbed an onion ring, blowing on the surface. Looking away from Joel and staring out at one of the crowded practice fields, full of middle-school kids chasing ground balls.

"I'm okay, I guess. I'm sure I could have managed to paddle around in a chair or whatever they use."

Joel's insides seemed to drop at least twenty degrees cooler than the early summer air around them.

"You could have? If you're not feeling up to it now, I completely understand."

The lie rolled out too easily by far. But with Duncan still looking away, Joel was too uneasy to try to take it back.

Duncan shrugged.

"I feel all right. I'm just not sure if it's a good idea, you know?"

All at once, the mouth-watering scents in front of Joel soured his stomach more than tempting it.

"I don't know, not really. I don't want to be pushy, but you did mention how swimming would be great therapy a few minutes ago. I'm getting worried I misunderstood something. Or did something. Or maybe *didn't* do something."

Joel gripped his own weary thigh under the table, vowing to keep his runaway mouth shut no matter how high his anxiety spiked.

Duncan ate his onion ring, then used another to push the rest of his food around on the blue paper plate.

"There's no way for me to say this that doesn't sound weird. Not that I can figure out, anyway." He closed his eyes, sighed, then finally looked back at Joel. "I think it would be better if I skip the movie."

Despite his grumbling stomach, Joel wished he hadn't eaten those fries. His mouth took advantage of the distraction.

"So something *did* go wrong."

Duncan's smile seemed friendly enough, but it had a sickly tinge.

"You're working pretty hard to figure out how to make this your fault, aren't you?"

Joel didn't need a mirror or anything else to know his face was turning bright red. He sat back and pushed his tray away.

"Force of habit, I guess. That and I don't have enough data or experience to come to any other conclusions."

Duncan's face fell into a miserable frown.

"Hey, I'm sorry. That didn't come out right at all. I didn't mean anything bad by it. It's just..."

He reached across the table to squeeze Joel's shoulder.

As much as he'd been daydreaming about Duncan touching a lot more than that, it was everything Joel could manage to keep from jerking away.

"You're not imagining things, Joel. I know this whole evening was my idea, and I wasn't exactly subtle about it. Maybe I was pushing too fast, you know? We hardly know each other, and we do need to keep working together. At least I hope we still can. We make a great team so far. I'd like to see how that goes."

After a couple of seconds that felt like an entire season, Joel decided to put on his very best fake smile. The idea of Duncan wanting to spend more time with him—and not just for socializing—didn't feel nearly as exciting as it had a few short minutes ago.

All he could catch hold of now was embarrassment busily working its way into shame. And more disappointment than he was able to deal with in public.

"Nothing to worry about, Duncan, not from my side. I figure a friendly turn at the batting cage is more of a social life than I've had for a while. Since I took this job, really. So what could I complain about? Better eat before our food gets too cold. Then we can both head out and do our own thing."

Duncan didn't look hurt, not exactly. He seemed more guilty and upset than anything else.

What had Joel heard his mother call a situation like this way back when he was in high school? Leading someone on?

Maybe Duncan had just realized he'd been leading Joel on, and wasn't as interested in more between them as he thought. And now he wanted to find a quick and easy way out of the rest of the evening.

It really was the least Joel could do.

And maybe the saddest part was he couldn't stop thinking about how much he needed Duncan as an assistant. Hopefully without a bunch of new discomfort and awkwardness between them, but he'd take what he could get.

He knew how to be lonely.

"Sounds good to me." Duncan picked up another onion ring. "This is too good to waste. So, in the interest of friendly co-worker dinner conversation, is Ms. Vincent as manic about other projects as she is about the parade float?"

The seriously delicious onion rings had somehow turned to sawdust in Duncan's mouth, but he forced himself to go on eating.

After the shitty way he'd just treated Joel, he could only hope his twisted and knotted stomach wouldn't reject every bite long before he got away from their painfully uncomfortable dinner and back to the sad shelter of his temporary apartment.

The sun dropping toward the horizon cooled the humid air, but nowhere near enough to make the idea of an evening swim less appealing. Any more than the idea of Joel in swim trunks had gotten less interesting after Duncan's ham-handed attempt to give them both a bit of safe distance.

Well, more to protect himself. From having to admit how underhanded and sneaky he was. And worse, from how much it would hurt when Joel finally figured out the truth.

And probably cut Duncan out of his life and never looked back.

Now all he had to do was get through the rest of the meal and hope he hadn't already messed up the entire situation.

Joel looked confused, and no wonder with the clunky question that had popped out of Duncan's mouth.

Nothing more than reverting to his long-ingrained spying habits.

And his even longer habit of blowing up relationships before they could even get started.

After a too-long moment of silent chewing, Joel washed a bite of his cheeseburger down and shrugged.

"I don't know if I'd say Ms. Vincent is manic about other projects. At least not since I've known her. Not as much as the float. But she's always kind of...intense."

"What's her story? Do you know much about her background?"

To keep himself from blurting out another question, Duncan took a huge bite of his own burger. Which was another damn shame, because he was sure it would taste fantastic if he hadn't spoiled his own appetite and Joel's too.

"I don't think anyone knows a whole lot about her," Joel said, face still tense and guarded. "I've heard rumors about shady investors who helped get Grateful Grocer started, but nothing anyone can prove. Typical for a small-town success story. More or less."

Duncan raised his eyebrows, intrigued despite his disappointment in how the evening was going.

Joel half smiled, but it didn't look remotely happy.

"Folks around town say she has a bunch of support from *out* of town, and that's how she gets such a big budget to work with. All I ever hear at work is the company is profitable, but maybe not enough to cover *all* the expenses. Like the investment in this place. I'm sure it brings in some money, and ad revenue and community goodwill and all that. I'm not in accounting, but I can't disagree that more seems to go out than comes in."

Duncan nodded, his interest perking up despite his all-too-familiar frustration with himself.

"I know I shouldn't dig where it's none of my business. I guess I'm just...trying to make conversation."

"Which we didn't have to do before now. Make conversation, I mean. Conversation just happened." Joel tilted his head to the side and looked at Duncan for a second before he went on. "Anyway, all I know is even the budget for that damn float is crazy, no matter how much attention it gets. Who knows? Maybe that's why she seems so wired all the time. Maybe she's hiding something."

"Or *afraid* of something."

Duncan was afraid his mouth had gotten away from him again when Joel blinked, then shook his head.

"Yeah, that could be it. She does kind of act like she's waiting for the bad news bomb to drop. Maybe we can suggest that to product development for their next coffee flavor."

Now it was Duncan's turn to put on a twisted smile.

"I can see the packaging you'll have to design for it. 'The Bad News Coffee Bomb. For days when caffeine alone won't do. Now with a secret hiding place for your spirit of choice built right in.'"

Joel snorted, happy to have a great chance to change the subject. "That or your *drug* of choice, hidden away in a specially made chamber right down the middle."

He rolled his eyes, but took a huge bite of his burger. Duncan realized his own appetite was recovering. The onion rings were almost as good warm as they had been hot.

"I'm sorry this all got so weird," he said. "Weird wasn't what I meant to happen at all. I was more trying to keep things from getting that way. I really did have a great time. Maybe we can do the movie another day. Or another round in the batting cage."

That got an almost normal laugh from Joel.

"Decide how you feel about that tomorrow. When you realize how many sore muscles you have."

Duncan held up both hands and flexed his fingers. They were stiff and tired, but still functional.

"Not too bad so far. I think I had enough fun to make it worthwhile. Thank you for teaching me how to bat."

Joel picked up a fry and twitched it back and forth like a scolding finger.

"You certainly got a decent look at hitting, and you did a great job. But I wouldn't say you're ready for live batting just yet. That machine goes up quite a few notches in speed, for one thing. And some of them can throw a reasonable curve ball, sure. All in pretty much the same spot, pitch after pitch. When it comes time for you to stand in against a real pitcher, you'll see the difference for sure."

"Not sure I'm ready for that just yet. Certainly not until you teach me how to throw and catch. I imagine I'll need to learn how to duck, too."

Joel shuddered. "That and how to stay in the box when someone's throwing at you, or just throwing wild. I remember that lesson better than I should. My uncle's idea of teaching us to stay put was to line a bunch of bats up right behind our feet, then throw high and inside. A couple of kids managed to jump backwards over all of them. I learned how to get tough enough to get hit and take my base without letting anyone know how much it hurt."

"We're probably back in the land of none of my business, but how old were you?"

"He rolled out that lesson for the first time when I was seven, maybe eight. Not that anyone was throwing hard enough to hurt back then. But by the time I got to high school, I could take a hard fastball without flinching. I had bruises on my shoulder or thigh that lasted more than a week. It's a wonder I never cracked a rib. But I got on base a lot, too."

Duncan's heart sank at the idea of such a young kid learning how to be that tough, to the point of willingly hurting himself when he got older.

Athlete Joel who'd shown up this afternoon was a hell of a lot more confident—and less anxious—than Work Joel. But Duncan was starting to see how they'd come from the same place.

"I hope you don't take this the wrong way, but your uncle sounds like kind of a jerk."

Joel laughed without a trace of the earlier uneasiness between them.

"You think? Now *that's* a lesson I understood long before I ever played baseball with the guy. What always blew my mind was how my father grew up with Uncle Greg and still thought it was a good idea for me to play on his team. I kinda got the idea Uncle Greg bullied Dad into it, but I'm still not sure who was the bigger jerk between the two of them. Wow, I haven't talked to anyone about this since I was that age and my whole team groused about it behind his back."

Duncan figured that made *him* the biggest jerk, since Joel had no idea this whole situation started out on a lie and kept going from there. But the one thing he wasn't faking was how much he liked Joel.

And how he liked him more by the minute.

"Glad I could help with that much, at least. Assuming talking about it helps."

Joel ate the last of his fries, and Duncan realized they'd both pretty much cleaned their plates after all.

"Sure, it helps," Joel said. "Same with talking about work. I wouldn't say Ms. Vincent is quite as hardass as Uncle Greg, but she often makes me feel like I barely missed getting hit by something. Sometimes like I took a direct hit to the head without a helmet. I guess for this job, I need to toughen up again."

Now Duncan's mind—and maybe a little of his heart— whipsawed right back to wanting to do whatever he could to help Joel, and to hell with his original reason for infiltrating Grateful Grocer in the first place.

Because Joel hadn't sounded like a grown-ass man just then, lamenting the frustrations of a tough boss during a stressful time at work.

He'd sounded and even looked like that eight-year-old learning how to be too tough, too young.

"I don't know about toughening up on the job," he said. "That's why I'm here in the first place, remember? To make things easier for you. So I say whatever happens tonight—or doesn't happen—we should concentrate on whatever it takes to make *that* happen. Deal?"

He picked up his second bottle of water and held it up.

"To whatever it takes?"

Joel hesitated for a few seconds, staring at Duncan in a way that made him feel like he was sitting there naked. And even more disconcerting, with his own head turned to glass and all his thoughts and motives and emotions made visible.

The biggest surprise of all was how some part of him *enjoyed* feeling that way.

"I'll meet you part of the way," Joel said, grabbing his bottle. "How about to whatever both of us can live with without burning out or driving ourselves crazy."

Chills that felt prickly and strange under sweat and warm night air raced across Duncan's arms. The background noise of thunks and pings, kids laughing, and adults cheering faded away.

Those words were uncomfortably close to the string of events that put him on this gig in the first place.

Maybe that meant he should take it to heart for a change, whether that meant work or personal stuff or anything else.

He nodded, and they both twisted off the lids, smiling at their weakened grips and tender skin.

"To whatever both of us can live with," Duncan said, "without burning out or driving ourselves crazy."

After swallowing half his water, Joel grinned.

"Since we're skipping swimming and the movie, we don't have to worry about eating too much. I don't know about you, but I could go for some ice cream. We could get it for free here, but there's a shop in town that's worth every penny. And every calorie. Maybe best of all, no affiliation with GG whatsoever. Parking is a bear on a Friday night, but we can drop our cars at work and walk if you're up for it."

"I can absolutely live with that. Ready when you are."

15

J oel wasn't sure whether it was the change of scenery, the cooler after-sunset air, or getting over his disappointment, but by the time he and Duncan got to The Chill Pad, he felt almost back to normal.

Main Street was packed as usual on a not-too-warm August Friday night. Families out strolling with varying numbers of kids and dogs, adult couples holding hands. Teenagers either roving in packs or paired off, giggling or staring moon-eyed at each other.

Kids old enough to get out mostly unsupervised but not yet dating, wandering and chattering, without a clue of the emotional turmoil gathering on their horizons.

All of them visiting or walking past a healthy array of small shops and eateries, enough to keep any one from getting too crowded.

Exhaust from a steady stream of cars cruising along the

wide street—mostly teenagers newly liberated from walking—was barely an undertone to the heady mix of pizza, roasting meat, popcorn, and other aromas that had to be piped outdoors on purpose.

Same with the friendly background of conversation, laughter, and soft music from doors propped open. The rumble of vehicles rolling by provided a pleasant counterpoint, with only a few stereos turned up loud enough to reach obnoxious levels.

Joel had strolled down here himself a few times since arriving in town.

Picking up a few odds and ends for the sweet little house he was finally starting to feel at home in. Sampling a surprising number of different good meals and snacks, especially for such a small, Midwestern town.

No doubt the influence of Grateful Grocer, pushing and helping local restaurants up their game considerably.

But until tonight, he'd wandered the street on his own every time.

Not for lack of options, even in a fairly small and gossipy office, and from around town in general. There were plenty of interested and interesting men and women to consider.

Still, a shy, anxious part of him held that side back, and had too often since he was one of those cruising teenagers.

It had always taken someone who surprised him with enough confidence and boldness to break through his protective reserve.

Someone like Duncan Jackson.

The big difference was Joel's unusual willingness to put

out a few hints of his own. He wasn't quite ready to use Duncan's reluctance to write the whole thing off.

Not just yet.

But Duncan's pushback, gentle though it had been, cooled Joel's fires considerably.

Thankfully the line at The Chill Pad wasn't too long, and they settled at a little round silver table by the window after only a few minutes. The whole place was either silver or black, including the light fixtures, with strings of tiny color-changing lights cycling through every hue, strung anywhere they would fit.

The usual groovy, lounge-type music went well with quiet conversation and an impressive range of flavors Joel had never seen anywhere else. Tonight he went with smoky cayenne mango sorbet, while Duncan went for a much more tradi-tional mint chocolate chip. Both presented in pre-chilled silvery dishes and metal spoons with insulated black handles.

But Joel was willing to bet most versions of that classic flavor weren't made with actual mint grown on a nearby herb farm, with enough mixed in to send its fresh, sharp aroma floating through the air.

"This is quite the scene for such a small town," Duncan said. "Has Stidham always been this lively?"

"I've only been here since the first of the year, so I can't say for sure. But this is about right any time there's nice weather on a Friday. Fourth of July was a madhouse, same as Memorial Day. They usually have some kind of concert or movie down at the square on Saturday nights, too."

Without saying a word, they both concentrated on their

double scoops. Joel's tasted and felt like he'd pulled a perfectly ripe mango out of the freezer, with the exact amount of heat to emphasize the sweetness.

"This is unreasonably good," Duncan said. "You've *got* to try it."

Before Joel could reply, Duncan got up—still moving a little slowly—and fetched two more spoons and little blue glasses of water.

Duncan winked as if he'd discovered a top-secret ice cream technique never before revealed to humankind. "They said they always give water with extra spoons. To clear the palate."

"This place is great enough that I'll take any advice they give me," Joel said.

Palate properly cleansed, Joel discovered the mint chocolate chip tasted as bright and fresh as it smelled, with dark-chocolate bits big and rich enough to hold their own.

"That's the problem with something this good," Duncan said. "I can't decide which is my favorite."

His gaze met Joel's with a return of the easy warmth they'd shared before, with enough heat mixed in to restore a little of Joel's earlier confidence.

"We'll have to keep trying until we find one we don't like. Might take a while since they change the flavors all the time."

Duncan grinned and switched back to his own ice cream.

"Sounds like a challenge I'd be a fool to resist, even if I wanted to."

Joel decided to go in a different direction while his boldness and Duncan's openness to it lasted.

But he did wait long enough for both of them to finish their ice cream, which wasn't very long at all.

"I want to ask you about something you said earlier."

Duncan raised his eyebrows and looked a little anxious.

"Not about me," Joel went on. "Or us. About Ms. Vincent."

Instead of seeming relieved, Duncan took a long, slow breath.

"Okay. Go ahead." He paused, then shook his head. "I'll answer if I can."

Joel didn't mean to frown, but it couldn't be helped. Duncan not being *able* to answer made no sense at all.

And that gave him all the more reason to keep going.

"The more I think about it," he said, "you weren't wrong when you said it seems like she's worried, or afraid of something. Hadn't occurred to me before, but it does kind of make sense. What did you mean? Or maybe I should ask what did you *see?*"

"Well, nothing really specific." Duncan looked down and fidgeted with his empty bowl, rolling it to one side, then the other. "It's more her general over-the-top, full-manic-speed-ahead sort of attitude. I haven't been here anywhere near long enough to know or even guess. But yeah, she makes me want to keep looking over my shoulder. So I ended up wondering if someone might be looking over hers."

Joel nodded, not willing to ignore his own unease in Ms. Vincent's presence.

"I haven't heard anyone else say much about her, but I'm not normally one for socializing at work. At least not at this job." He shrugged and smiled. "I guess I usually do get to know people besides my much-appreciated assistant. Most places I haven't been nearly so slammed. Now that I'm paying attention, I wonder how high she'd jump at a loud noise."

"That's another thing," Duncan said, looking up. "Am I imagining that she *enjoys* startling people? I mean, I suppose we were the surprise visitors to the break room the other day, but she seemed delighted at almost running us down."

Joel rolled his eyes. "I'm sure you noticed she has a habit of lurking right outside my office whenever she can. I couldn't tell you how many times I've jumped halfway out of my skin because she's just *there*. Watching me. And I have no idea for how long."

"Wonder if she does that to everyone else?"

"She might if they were in charge of the almighty most important marketing stunt of the year." Joel rubbed his eyes with fingers still cool from his bowl. "No, that's not really fair. I appreciate her trusting me with the float design, and I'll probably have fun with it once we really get started. I definitely appreciate her letting me get help, which I very much needed."

Duncan leaned forward with a crooked grin and mock bow.

"I appreciate the opportunity myself. And, the whole setup does seem kinda...off somehow. Not that I don't want to do what I can to help, especially if that means spending time hitting things to let off steam. The intrigue angle only makes the whole work situation more interesting, you know?"

"That's one way to look at it," Joel said. "One of the

reasons I stayed freelance for so long was to keep things lively for myself. I'd get to know the town, the job, the people, and be ready to move on a few months later. Some of my friends from school have had the same job since right after graduation." He shrugged and spun his own empty bowl on the table. "Not much of a recipe for long-term security, I guess."

"What made you decide to take full-time at Grateful Grocer?"

Joel laughed, knowing his cheeks were turning red again.

"Honestly? What we were just talking about. Ms. Vincent offered me an insane salary, and off-the-chart benefits. Including help with housing, not that Stidham is a particularly expensive market. All the training I can jam into my skull, too. I guess I'm getting to the age where that kind of opportunity and security are tough to pass up."

Duncan stared up at Joel's favorite feature in The Chill Pad: solid-black, mirrored disco balls.

But the tension around his eyes and mouth when he looked back stirred up more unease in Joel's otherwise pleasantly full belly.

"I've had plenty of opportunity and security when it comes to work, and more than my fair share of challenges and excitement. Funny thing is, I've been looking for a change of pace myself. In the opposite direction. A stretch of peace and quiet sounds good to me, with enough change to keep me engaged, maybe. If that's even possible."

Joel refused to let the worrier side of his personality turn that difference between their current states of mind into a negative. No matter their reasons, they'd both ended up at GG at the same time.

Even if his romantic curiosity about Duncan eventually went nowhere, having a new friend couldn't possibly be a bad thing.

"A small-town job with an energetic boss might suit you better than you think," Joel said. "Who knows? We might round up enough interest to get a Grateful Grocer softball team together. That should keep you challenged."

Duncan groaned.

"We'll see about *that* after I find out how sore I'm going to be in the morning. But I'm certainly intrigued by the possibilities around here so far. All of them."

Joel sternly ordered the slow, warm flip-flops in his chest to cool it, but he couldn't keep from smiling right back at Duncan.

"So am I."

16

Despite unreasonably sore thighs, hips, back, and backside—worse on Sunday than Saturday—Duncan was moving more or less normally by a gray, rainy Monday morning.

The simple ability to walk upright without grunting or staggering felt like a huge victory.

One he attributed to alternating rounds of ice packs, hot baths, and carefully separated doses of ibuprofen and whiskey.

And none of that had been as bad as his guilt over pushing Joel into talking about Ms. Vincent after stirring up a sticky brew of questions and suspicions.

He paused before stepping into Joel's office, quite aware he was edging way too close to Ms. Vincent's lurking habits.

Because the worst part of all—and what kept him from sleeping even more than his quarreling muscles—was how

109

rotten he felt about giving Joel such a cold push-off Friday night. When all Duncan himself had wanted to do was go home with Joel and forget all about the spy nonsense.

He took a deep breath and kept going.

The heavy, overcast sky changed the focus in Joel's office, shifting it away from the vibrant downtown scene outside the huge widows and toward the islands of light over his desk.

No glaring tubes behind dull white panels here.

Joel hadn't said whether he insisted on the subtle, far more natural light sources up there or not. Duncan hadn't been interested enough in anyone else's desk to pay attention to whether they were more traditional.

Maybe not, with the fabulous wall of plants in the break room.

Today, those soft spotlights worked to make Joel the most vivid and interesting thing in sight, as if he weren't already in Duncan's eyes.

Joel stood in front of the four big corkboards the two of them had set up Friday, arms crossed and unmoving.

He'd broken his own typical dress code by wearing black jeans, which did a hell of a lot more for his athletic backside than his khakis ever could. His unfairly sexy legs were covered, but Duncan could too easily imagine them now. Probably just as well Joel stayed with one of his geek-forward dress shirts neat and tucked rather than the casual t-shirt that emphasized his arms.

Before Duncan could figure out what the dark blue pattern marching across the black fabric was, Joel turned and saw him.

And his smile made up for the lack of sunshine outside and then some.

"*There* you are. I was getting worried you'd call in sore this morning."

Duncan snorted. "And let you think I'm that easy to break down? I have to point out I'm only on time, instead of my usual early appearance. Anyway, I would have crawled in here if I had to."

"I'm glad it didn't come to that. Seriously, how you feeling?"

"Much better today than yesterday. That was kind of an ugly scene." Duncan tucked his bag under the desk and stood beside Joel. "But I will admit Henry the building supervisor was concerned about why I was walking like someone at least twice my age. You?"

"Told you Henry doesn't miss much. He asked me if I'd had a rough weekend, too. I'll be more honest with you than I was with him, and just say I had my share of discomfort and leave it at that."

Duncan waved one hand toward the collections of images they'd narrowed the Tsunami of Bad Ideas down to.

"Find your starting point yet?"

"For the float? Not just yet. But we'll get it locked down this week." Joel glanced over his shoulder, then stepped closer to Duncan. Almost close enough to touch. "I *did* spend some time thinking about the other project we discussed on Friday. I think there's a lot to work with there. And a lot more that probably won't be all that hard to uncover."

Duncan decided to give himself credit for the fact that he

felt guilty about dragging Joel into this *before* his normal spy-gig curiosity kicked in.

"That project might be a bit high-risk, and possibly low-reward. If any reward at all."

Joel shrugged and turned away from the corkboards to look at Duncan, his blue eyes curious and excited.

"True. But I've been thinking a lot about how high the risk might be if I don't look into it at all. This kind of project might eventually undermine my newly stable situation before it really gets started if I ignore it, you know?"

Duncan rubbed the back of his neck, letting that change of perspective sink in.

He'd only focused on his own benefits from this gig at first, until he got to know Joel. Then he'd spent all his allotted fretting time concentrating on how much trouble Joel could get into, either by having the triple-damned float design leak, or by digging too much into the CEO's possibly shady connections.

He hated to admit it, even to himself, but he hadn't considered the potential damage to Joel if Grateful Grocer collapsed under its own questionable finances. Not to mention to a good-sized workforce here at headquarters and in the growing number of stores.

He hadn't exactly built a successful career as a corporate spy type on worrying too much about the consequences of his investigations. The fact that he normally exited the scene before the fallout arrived had protected him quite nicely.

Duncan couldn't deny the poetic justice of deciding to take a break from that career—what he'd foolishly thought would be a break, anyway—and ending up in the first situation he might not *want* to disappear from.

That shift hardly brought Duncan into savior territory, but maybe it nudged him out of evildoer just enough.

"Okay, I see your point," he said. "Especially since you've decided to jump into this particular project long-term. It's always a good idea to know as much as you can in a situation like that."

Joel chuckled. "Yeah, I guess I should have thought that through before I made my commitment. I'm hoping that old cliche about better late than never applies here."

"I hope so too."

They both jumped at an alarmingly boisterous cackle from outside Joel's office door.

Duncan started to turn, but Joel grabbed his arm.

"No, just stay here," he said, not much above a whisper. "Wouldn't hurt to show off all our progress, right?"

"I guess if she's laughing, we can assume she's not lurking."

Bonnie Vincent spoke from the doorway then, in her usual borderline-manic tones.

"Looks like you boys are finally getting something done. I almost didn't recognize your office, Joel. Who knew there was a desk under all those piles of clutter?"

Joel turned, and Duncan did the same a beat later.

This morning, Ms. Vincent sported a less golf-oriented outfit, instead going with a more nautical theme. Her navy-blue topsider shoes matched her white-stitched button-up shirt, with sleeves rolled up in ironed-sharp creases to just above her elbows. The brown slacks had a sort of satiny look, as if they'd be water-resistant enough to withstand the rain outside and waves crashing over the deck as well.

She'd shed the tennis bracelet, but a charm bracelet with bejeweled boat anchors and fish and such probably cost almost as much.

"Good morning, Ms. Vincent," Joel said. "We've definitely gotten things under control, mainly thanks to Duncan's organizing skills. We should have preliminary designs ready for you to look at this week."

Ms. Vincent stood beside them, and Duncan could have sworn she was wearing some sort of ocean-breeze-scented perfume.

"I have to admit I'm not sure where you're going with these, Joel." All traces of her usual over-the-top enthusiasm had vanished. Now she only sounded confused, with annoyed coming up fast behind. "I can't make sense of it. What are they, color coded?"

Duncan stared at the boards, fighting off an urge to tell her to mind her own freaking business and wait until her very skilled designer was good and damn ready to explain it to her. Sounded way too much like his grouchy grandfather for anyone's good.

He and Joel had put the reasonable design suggestions together by theme, not color, especially since several of them were black-and-white or faded newsprint-yellow. A cool retro theme with a Fifties vibe, an old-fashioned bounty-of-the-Earth kind of thing more from the Seventies, a sort of Nineties excess-is-good focus, and an almost spare modern take.

Joel only smiled.

"There's some color coding, sure," he lied, as smoothly as Duncan could have in pure spy mode. "Like I said, Duncan has a great knack for getting things organized so I...so *we* can take a good look at our options."

Ms. Vincent cocked her head one way, then the other, tapping her fingers against her thigh so the ostentatious charm bracelet tinkled.

"Well, you've come up with good designs for us so far. I guess I have a hard time thinking at this kind of basic level. You know, seeing all the small pieces before they can possibly fit together."

She smacked her thigh, rattling the charms and setting Duncan's teeth on edge.

The jarring exuberance in her voice roared back full force to match.

"And *that's* why we hired you, right? Both of you. I'll get out of your hair and let you get back to it since time's wasting. The big event's just around the corner." She pointed to the neat stacks on one side of Joel's desk. "Need me to send someone to gather all of the rejects?"

Joel shook his head.

"We're not sure they're rejects just yet, Ms. Vincent. We've got plenty of inspiration, thanks to you, so no need to put out another call for ideas. It's just too soon in the process to turn any of what we already have away. You never know what might bubble up to the top before it's all said and done."

He looked into Duncan's eyes, and the determination there made it clear Joel had already made up his mind.

At least when it came to snooping into Ms. Vincent and Grateful Grocer's background.

"Then carry on, boys, carry on."

She charged out of the office as if the floor was the up-tilted deck of a ship, jingling her wrist the whole way.

Joel let out his customary breath when they heard Ms. Vincent turning her intense attention toward some other poor Monday-morning soul.

"You were more direct with her than usual," Duncan said. "I'm not sure whether that's a good or bad thing."

Joel's grin made it clear he was leaning toward good.

"I'm not sure yet either. I guess we'll find out, huh?"

17

By the time the Monday slog ended, Joel had managed to get his overstimulated nervous system more or less calmed down.

But before that, he'd spent most of the day alternating between worry about Ms. Vincent saying she couldn't make sense of what they were doing, and a sizzle closer to terror about more-or-less admitting to Duncan how he wanted to dig into her background.

Into the whole company's background was more like it.

He didn't bother pretending to himself that his agitation wasn't affecting his work. Duncan kept bringing Joel's attention back to whatever they were trying to do. Politely, and without being the least bit snotty about it, which were major points in his favor.

The fact that Duncan never came right out and asked

what the hell the problem was made it clear he already had a good idea.

Mainly because of Duncan—and his willingness to keep bringing Joel back from the potential panic inside his head—they did manage to make a good start on four basic designs before the end of the long, rainy day.

Remembering that he was likely dragging Duncan into a possibly illegal and certainly unethical mess only kept Joel's nerves frazzled and stretched to their limits.

At not too long past their normal quitting time, Duncan stood and pushed his chair back, as he had several times throughout the day. He stretched his arms up, moved them out to the side, then slowly dropped into a deep squat, hugging his knees.

It was the deep, satisfied groan while he was down there that got to Joel, every single time.

"Finally starting to feel better?" Joel said, pretending to keep most of his attention on his monitor.

"I'll count being able to do that at all as a major improvement. I could barely stand up straight Saturday. Those are starting to look good. Do we need to print them out for anyone else to see?"

Joel shivered.

"Oh, let's please perish *that* thought. The last thing we want to do is invite an endless stream of commentary before we have something solid enough to back up. If we show anyone something this rough—especially Ms. Vincent—it's like handing out red ink pens and demanding they find problems. Because they will. Trust me."

"Makes sense to me. But I like what you've got so far. That's got to count for something, right?"

A far more pleasant tingle started from Joel's belly and worked its way out to more sensitive parts. He returned Duncan's shy smile.

"That counts for a lot."

Joel was partial to the modern, stylized design with outlines of colorful fruit, vegetables, and other kitchen staples like eggs, milk, and chicken. He was pretty sure Duncan preferred one that was basically a miniature functioning grocery store on wheels, complete with shelves and freezer cases and plenty of room for impulse aisle items like candy bars and magazines. All to be strategically handed out along the parade route, naturally.

Of course their own favorites wouldn't matter at all, whether they tried to juice the presentation in their favor or not.

The approval of only one person would make the difference. And Joel had no guesses whatsoever about what would draw Ms. Vincent's eye when the time came.

That thought turned Joel's nervous engine back up into the red, and his mouth took over before his mind could try and hit the brakes.

"Listen, you busy for dinner? My treat, since I'll probably talk your ears off."

Duncan slung his bag over his shoulder and cocked his head. He looked more curious than amorous, and that was probably for the best.

"Not busy at all. Depending on what you want to talk

about, a restaurant might not be the best choice. My apartment looks like a sitcom set from about twenty years ago, but it's nice. I'm not a gourmet chef by any means, but I'll do my best if you're not too picky."

"I'm not all that picky," Joel said, "but I'd be glad to get takeout. Less dishes, stress, and mess that way. Your choice, within reason. Stidham has more than most small towns for sure. I can recommend pizza, Italian, Chinese, and a decent seafood place, believe it or not. Great burger joint if you want, too."

They walked toward the front of the building together. The lobby functioned more as a Grateful Grocer ad campaign than a typical corporate headquarters entryway.

The walls were covered with bright, honestly mouth-watering images of ripe produce, gorgeous breads and decorated cakes, and a holiday-worthy spread of family tables groaning with perfectly baked meats, fish, and all the side dishes any American could possibly want.

A coffee station almost as fancy as the one in the break room waited across from a row of unusually welcoming couches and chairs, all done in GG colors, of course. This time of day, only a couple of the carafes were still out and surely full of steaming hot brain juice. The rest sat gleaming and polished, ready for the morning.

A sleek red receptionist's desk in the middle of the room was generally empty unless Very Important Visitors were expected, and today was no exception. Instead of anything so formal, Henry the friendly-but-sharp building supervisor sat at a much smaller wooden desk beside the front door.

He grinned and got to his feet when Joel and Duncan approached.

Henry had to be in his early sixties judging from his curly silver hair and network of smile lines around his face. But his well-over-six-feet-tall frame was still quite strong, and probably not that much different from his obviously athletic youth.

Joel couldn't stop himself from wondering just how far Henry could knock a baseball if he got a good read on it. His light blue eyes always had the sharp focus of someone who didn't miss much.

"Heading out for a big night?" Henry had the flat, sort of nasal local accent more than Joel or Duncan did.

"Heading out for dinner and a much-needed break, Henry," Joel said. "Has anyone properly introduced you to Duncan Jackson yet?"

Henry stepped forward and shook Duncan's outstretched hand.

"Not in so many words," Henry said. "But I've seen him around. Henry Koen, glad you're here, Duncan. Joel sure can use the help around here with so much coming his way. Looks like you're walking a lot better than you were this morning."

Duncan laughed and nodded.

"Starting to recover, yes. Joel took me out to the batting cage and taught me how to hit a baseball or maybe a hundred on Friday. Still feeling the effects."

Henry nodded, still smiling.

"That'll do it. I was more of a wrestler and basketball player myself, but I sure know how hard it can knock you back if you've been away from it for a while. You two have a good dinner, now. I'll be off for my own soon enough."

"Will do," Joel said. "Once Duncan decides what he wants to eat."

All three of them laughed, and Duncan aimed a not-too-hard elbow at Joel's side.

"Takeout works for me," Duncan said, "and I could go for pizza if they've got good thin-crust."

"Assuming we agree on what that means, they have a good one. Ever had Imo's, over toward St. Louis?"

Duncan shook his head as they stepped out into the hot, impossibly muggy afternoon. The rain had stopped for the moment, but Joel thought the humidity must be at least a hundred and ten percent. The soppy air made the fresh scent of happy grass and trees quite a bit less appealing.

"Let me just say this isn't like Imo's," Joel said, "which is more or less like cheese on a cracker. Great if you grew up there and that's what you want. Probably weird if you've never had it before. This will be good and crispy. Let me know what toppings you want, and I can pick it up on the way over to your apartment. Better yet, I can go ahead and order delivery so we won't have to wait. Do I need to grab drinks?"

"I've got soda, beer, and mixers for the more powerful stuff." Duncan stopped on the sidewalk and crossed his arms. "Salad too, if you're good with Italian dressing. You sure you want to get into this, Joel? I don't mean dinner. That sounds like fun, even if all we do is chat and maybe watch a movie. I mean all the rest. The project we discussed Friday."

"I'm sure I at least want to..." Joel waved one hand in the

air, searching for both words and feelings. "I don't know, talk about it. See if what I've been thinking makes sense outside my own head. You comfortable with that?"

"Comfortable enough for dinner." Duncan shrugged. "Talking doesn't get anyone into trouble most of the time. As long as no one overhears when you don't want them to."

Joel started walking again, Duncan falling into step beside him.

Unlike the last time the two of them planned dinner together, Joel's mind wasn't full of decidedly adult images that were very much not safe for work.

This time, he kept thinking of Ms. Vincent lurking and sneaking up on him, even before he had an assistant to talk to. The absurd hours he'd worked on projects that even she didn't think were nearly as important as this damn parade.

The constant underhanded comments and remarks she said right in front of him, with no telling what she said to everyone else.

His own puzzlement over how Grateful Grocer operated the way it did, with a seemingly endless flow of resources coming in that couldn't possibly be explained by their sales.

Maybe most of all, the fact that he couldn't remember Ms. Vincent ever sincerely thanking him, or saying he'd done a good job. Not one damn time.

"Good. Then dinner it is," he said. "And plenty of talking to go with it."

18

Duncan tried to keep from slipping into a panic as he opened his apartment door, Joel waiting right behind him.

Not because they would be so close to his bedroom, even though he'd had plenty of thoughts about spending time there with Joel. And not even because he was afraid Joel was going to talk himself into trouble before the evening was over.

Instead Duncan was struck by a rather school-kid certainty that he'd left something truly foul in the sink, or a gigantic pile of filthy underwear had somehow manifested itself in the middle of the living room floor.

He'd actually been a fairly neat kid who'd turned into an even neater adult, most of the time. This odd agitation surely came from stress involving his non-standard laptop loaded with a highly suspicious number of investigator and spy tools. He knew he'd remembered to stow it safely in the bedroom, with security to match the contents in the locked case and more tightly locked computer.

He still paused halfway through the door for a quick look before stepping aside.

"Remembered to hide everything this morning?" Joel said, grinning as he walked inside.

"As far as I can see from here. No promises about the rest. I didn't have anywhere near enough warning to do much about the somewhat outdated decor."

Joel stood beside the earth-tone, pillow-piled couch, hands on his hips, shaking his head.

The living room was only separated from the kitchen by a set of chest-high tan block-and-board shelves packed full of dusty LPs, pristine hardcover books that were mostly non-fiction, and vintage board games a little battered around the edges.

"You weren't kidding about the sitcom set," Joel said. "Some of this stuff could be from the *Eighties*. Whoever you're renting from either has a huge dedication to tracking these peculiar collector's items down, or they've taken amazing care of it for a long time."

Duncan got a couple of mismatched glasses off an open shelf, one muddy brown, the other muted green.

"After checking out the cabinets in here, I'm going with an endless stream of thrift shop treasures. Quite sustainable and economical, and no worries about fitting into a decorating scheme. Or breaking a plate and ruining a set. Want something to drink before the pizza gets here?"

"I suppose I should be good on an empty stomach and go

with water. Cold, or with ice if you have it, since it's even more miserable than usual out there."

Duncan grabbed a few perfectly square cubes from the tan refrigerator's ice maker.

"Tap okay? It tastes really good here."

Joel nodded as he wandered toward the little rectangle of a kitchen table, peering at everything along the way. The table seemed to confirm Duncan's idea about broken plates and such. The top was made of various bits and pieces of ceramic, metal, glass, even flat stones, all of it held in place with a thin layer of pale-yellow grout.

"Tap works for me, despite all the brilliant ad designs I've done all about the superior flavor and quality of GG bottled water. Did you meet whoever lives here, or owns it? I'd love to know their story."

Duncan joined Joel at the table with both glasses full of water and bobbing ice cubes.

"No idea who they are, but I'd like to know more about them myself. Watch out, there are a couple of hidden sharp edges."

Joel snorted out a laugh, then covered his mouth. He couldn't hide his red cheeks.

"Sorry, that wasn't exactly what I meant to do. Well, I *never* mean to snort, but it sneaks its way out. Just the idea of hidden edges hit me funny after the way our Friday went, and me deciding to abandon my lifelong good-employee facade and maybe drag you with me into the abyss."

Duncan took a long drink, hoping his guilt didn't show on his own face. Over his behavior on Friday, yeah. But he wasn't feeling especially good about giving Joel more than a few suggestions on the road toward spyhood.

"Sharp edges does kind of fit, doesn't it? So, want to tell me what you've been thinking about, or do you need something stronger to drink for that?"

"Probably better if I get it out now," Joel said. "Before I lose my nerve. Honestly, I've wondered from day one how the hell Grateful Grocer manages their books. Along with how they manage all the local sponsorships, and all that research and development. One reason I'm here is the salary they offered ticks over the line into outrageous, too."

He took a drink, watching Duncan the whole time, before going on.

"Between that and Ms. Vincent's whole one-breath-away-from-screaming persona, I can't pretend I'm not suspicious."

Duncan did a better job of keeping his face and voice calm than he expected to.

"I think that's reasonable. The whole setup struck me as odd almost from the beginning, too. You have something in mind to do about it?"

Joel tapped one short, neat fingernail on a shard of bright pink glass on the tabletop.

"This is where it gets tricky, or it will if I actually go through with anything. I'm not any kind of accountant, or much of a computer whiz outside of graphic design. But I *do* seem to have an old laptop from someone in accounting, or maybe legal. Not my usual work rig, that one's brand new. But GG gave me a travel computer for a conference they sent me to St. Louis for when I first started, so I could take notes. Before my real one was ready."

Duncan tried not to hold his breath, and his face felt stiff and hot from trying so hard not to show any reaction.

"You think the laptop has the wrong permissions set up?"

"I figured you'd know the way to say it and make sense," Joel said. "When I logged in to that machine, I saw shortcuts for a bunch of servers I didn't recognize pop up on the desktop. They wouldn't work at the conference hotel, of course. But they did work when I got back. As soon as I logged in at the office."

Now Duncan's heart sped up enough that he was afraid his voice would shake with the high tempo.

"You said you *have* that computer. Does that mean no one took it back?"

Joel nodded slowly, his gaze locked with Duncan's.

"Like I said, it's an old machine. The contractor who gave it to me apologized the whole time. I could get online and take notes with it, but thankfully it wasn't a graphics training class where I'd need to use high-powered software. I doubt I could have even launched Photoshop with the poor beast. My new machine showed up on my desk right after I got back. No one ever asked me to return the creaky old loaner."

Duncan balled up his fists on his thighs, not sure whether to let his spy-self take total control. That part of him was quick, and clever, and most of all, exhilarating and exciting.

But it could also charge ahead way too fast, without paying attention to who might get hurt. Not fast enough to get caught, mind you. Otherwise he wouldn't have lasted weeks in the job, much less all these years.

That little trait accounted for much of Duncan's success, as well as his recent battle with burnout.

"Sounds to me like no one ever wiped the hard drive before they turned it into a loaner," he said. "That, or it was imaged for someone in accounting or legal or even HR, and never re-imaged later. If you decide to go through with this, a computer like that would be quite handy to have."

"I thought it might. That's why I kept it at home instead of turning it in. That and the irresistible lure of having a secret, you know?"

Duncan reached out and carefully rubbed his finger along one of those sharp edges—a slightly upturned bit of what looked like the curved part of a daisy-covered plate.

Joel had just described a huge part of what got Duncan into the spy game to begin with.

Having those secrets himself, and *taking* those secrets from companies that wanted to keep them.

"Yeah, I do know," he said. "Probably too well for my own good. Assuming you decide to do anything with that laptop, how confident are you that someone in IT won't be watching for it to connect?"

Joel breathed deep and let out a long sigh, one of the habits Duncan enjoyed more than he should. Like the way Joel's gaze carried a heat all its own.

"I already decided, Duncan. I think having an outsider see how weird my work situation really is forced me to see it too." His serious expression shifted into a smile, but his gaze didn't falter. "Anyway, you missed an important point. GG was expanding almost all its departments when I came on board. The *contractor* who gave me that laptop is long gone. I'd say odds are good the person who took over never knew it existed."

Duncan blinked, surprised at himself for missing a detail like that. Seemed mixing work with pleasure, and guilt with desire, softened his usual skills more than he realized.

"I did miss that, you're right. Did you bring it with you?"

Joel somehow managed to turn a simple nod with eye contact into an outrageously sexy move.

"Put it in my car this morning after not touching it for months. I told you I thought about this all weekend. Not sure I can get into the work network with it, since I haven't tried since that time at the conference hotel, and once at work when I got back. But I get into everything fine from home with my regular laptop."

"When you're not using a public connection. That can make a difference with a secure logon." Duncan paused, but only for a second. For better or worse, the excited light in Joel's eyes was too enticing to resist. "Okay, I won't ask you again if you're sure, even though I feel like I should. I *will* ask why you decided to bring the laptop."

19

Joel did his level best to keep from fidgeting, at least where Duncan would see. But the urge to tap his foot, or drum his fingers on the adorably awful tabletop, or maybe even slip back into a long-abandoned habit of cracking his knuckles was nearly impossible to resist.

Hell, he was a breath away from getting up to investigate more of the neat but seriously overcrowded apartment. None of the weirdly mismatched knickknacks were Duncan's, any more than the books, huge collection of DVDs, or the section of one wall dedicated to an unhealthy number of scarves were.

But that didn't stop Joel's curiosity, or his uncertainty over how to answer Duncan's seemingly simple question.

Joel had never breathed a word about the ancient loaner laptop, not since the day he'd gotten back to the office and seen the shiny new replacement waiting on his desk.

Not because he was trying to be especially sneaky, or

wanted to score a free computer. The loaner truly was quite the dinosaur, at least compared to his fully loaded beast of a machine.

He'd barely thought about it at all.

Not even when he'd slung the scuffed and creased bag that came with it over his shoulder and taken it right back home that same afternoon.

He watched Duncan, who made no effort to hide his own nervous movement.

In the last few seconds, he'd shifted in his seat, ruffled his hair, and rubbed at a random bit of crockery embedded in the table.

Joel would just have to spit it out and let Duncan twitch for both of them.

"This will sound lame," he said, "probably because it is. I'd pretty much forgotten all about the rusty old thing until... Well, until I laid down on the floor at home to try to stretch my hips. You know how you pull one knee up toward your chest, then lean it over toward the opposite side?"

Duncan nodded, a tiny smile curving his lips in a most interesting way.

"Anyway," Joel said, "when I did that in the living room, I saw the beat-up bag the laptop was in. And with what we'd been talking about, I remembered those network shortcuts. After a few more hours of all the bizarre things about Grateful Grocer percolating through my brain, I grabbed it on my way out the door this morning."

"But not so you could turn it in at long last and clear your guilty conscience."

Joel let out a breathy laugh, and a good chunk of his tension went with it.

"That never even crossed my mind. I figured since no one's realized it's missing, or that *I* have it, no one would likely notice if I booted it up again. Or if I launched those shortcuts again, assuming they work anymore."

Now Duncan's lips pulled over to one side, and he shrugged.

"There are a bunch of *ifs* there, depending on how well records were kept during the IT transition and whether a good inventory was done before that. Also, there's a question of how good GG's internal network security is. But it's possible we could do that, sure. What would you be looking for if we did?"

Something in Duncan's manner—and in his questions—set off a tingle of warning in Joel's mind. But not the kind of warning that made him want to get away, or even stop talking.

This was more the kind of warning that he might be understood better than he expected.

And he quite liked that possibility.

Almost as much as he liked Duncan referring to the two of them as *we*.

"It did cross my mind that we might learn something about where GG got the startup money," Joel said. "Or maybe where they get what does seem like too much consistent income now. Or, possibly we might learn a thing or two about Ms. Vincent while we're at it."

"Makes sense. Assuming we can get in at all, I'd say it would be worth starting there."

Joel's phone buzzed in his pocket, and he glanced at his watch for the message.

"Our dinner's here. But don't think I missed you saying *starting* just now. Don't answer now, just take a minute to think about it while I get the food. Why do I get the feeling this wouldn't be your first rodeo when it comes to digging into things you're not supposed to know?"

Duncan reached across the little table, grabbed Joel's wrist, and smiled.

"I think I'll go get it, since I live here. You bought, so I'll handle the tip. Make yourself at home." He got up and headed toward the door before Joel could respond, but turned back. "Or, grab that laptop if you want. We can work out our plan of attack while we eat."

Joel called out before Duncan managed to close the door.

"An unanswered question only draws more attention to itself!"

Duncan's laugh was the only answer.

With Joel nearly sprinting after him and racing back upstairs with the laptop, they got back at about the same time.

"Yours smells a hell of a lot better than mine," Joel said. His next breath got caught up in trying to suppress yet another snorting laugh.

Duncan put a huge white cardboard box on the blue-tiled kitchen counter, explaining the divine aroma of onions, garlic, and general pizza paradise. All Joel carried was a black faux-leather bag that looked like it had been kicked and stepped on frequently, maybe while shoved under cramped airplane seats.

"That thing does look like it's been used as a doorstop," Duncan said. "But does it really have a smell?"

Joel made a production of holding the bag up close to his nose in several different spots.

"You know, it does have kind of a musty stink. Like no one remembers it exists, which is more than a little pitiful."

Duncan peeked inside the box and took a deep breath, then turned to tuck it into the stainless-steel wall oven already set to keep their dinner warm. He leaned against the counter and gazed at Joel with one eyebrow raised.

"Or maybe that's the accumulated fragrance of a long-held secret?" Duncan said. "One that's about to get put into play?"

Now the tingle in Joel's mind settled in his chest and belly, and it took on a warmer, more excited flavor. Not all that different from how he'd felt watching Duncan work out how to get his hips into the swing on Friday.

"Seems to me secrets can have a peak season," Joel said. "Kind of like a bottle of wine. Open one too early, and you won't get everything out of it that you could have. Wait too long, and the whole thing starts to go sour."

Duncan raised both eyebrows, and the flirty light went out of his eyes and his voice.

"The last thing we want is a bottle full of vinegar, unless it's for salad. Hang on, I'll get the bowls."

He turned away, leaving Joel staring at his back. Not a bad perspective at all, especially when he reached up to get two big bowls and hiked up his shirt enough to show a naughty peek of skin.

But that response and retreat turned up Joel's interest this time instead of damping it down.

"Let me help." Joel stepped around the counter just as Duncan opened the refrigerator door. "Wow, you weren't kidding about having salad stuff."

Duncan laughed but didn't look at Joel.

The fridge wasn't all that full, but an impressive number of Grateful Grocer's clever vegetable holders took up a lot of space. Each one was made of bumpy brown cardboard with little windows built in all around. All the parts—even the windows—were biodegradable and could be brought back to stores for that purpose.

"Yeah, once I realized my work badge got me a discount, I kind of stocked up. Hit a great farmers market, too. As long as we don't both like exactly the same things, there should be plenty."

"I'm fine with everything but raw radishes," Joel said, lining up the boxes on the counter around the bowls. "Same with garlic and red onions. They're fine when they're cooked, but they tear me up otherwise."

Duncan wasn't kidding about stocking up. Joel had his choice of pre-sliced bell peppers in red, orange, and yellow, two varieties of mushrooms, and both red and green cabbage. There were also three different kinds of lettuce to go with shredded carrots, chopped celery, and red and yellow beets.

"I've got fruit too," Duncan said. "Tangerines, cherries, a few fresh blueberries. A few different kinds of olives, and capers. Walnuts, sunflower seeds, pecans. I can toast those if you want."

Joel grabbed a set of tongs out of an oversized canister decorated to look like a rocket ship. It was stuffed full of all kinds of kitchen tools, including some he didn't know the name or use for.

"I think I'll be fine with what you've got out already. Most salad bars aren't this well stocked."

Duncan flashed a shy smile.

"I guess I like busy salads. That and I never get bored. There are a few bottled dressings in the fridge, and good bottles of olive oil and vinegar in the cabinet."

By the time they managed to put together appropriately nutritious and colorful salads without fighting over ingredients, Joel was apologizing for his grumbling belly. A few minutes of companionably silent eating took the edge off.

No matter how conflicted he felt about working there, he couldn't possibly fault GG for the quality of their produce. Every bite was crisp and fresh and delicious.

"Now that I've got a solid dose of the healthy stuff on board," Joel finally said, "I'm ready for pizza. And a little more conversation, if you're up for it."

Duncan stared into Joel's eyes long enough that Joel's cheeks heated up once again.

"I suppose we have a few things to discuss if we're going to crack into that laptop. Starting with what you plan to do if we find anything."

20

Duncan got up to get the pizza, and to give Joel a chance to think about how he wanted to answer.

Assuming he didn't dodge the question the same way Duncan had.

The box was plenty warm and smelled outrageously good. He expected he'd easily be able to overcome his lingering pangs of guilt enough to manage to eat.

As long as he didn't think too much about what Joel was getting himself into. And more quickly than he would have without help from Duncan.

A clatter behind him made it clear Joel was doing his part to get the feast on the table. He'd scooped up the empty salad bowls, stacked them in the sink, and fetched two plates. One white with blue flowers around the edges, the other solid yellow.

"Need a fork?" Joel said. "Or do you eat with your fingers like a civilized man?"

"When the food and the situation demand it. And this certainly does. I say it's time for a beer as well. Care to join me?"

"I didn't *quite* feel comfortable grabbing one for myself, so thank you for asking."

Their eyes met, and Duncan knew he was in trouble no matter what Joel decided about the aged laptop.

It would be a hell of a lot harder to cut and run from his own apartment than it had been from the batting cages. Not that he wanted to this time, no matter how much he *knew* this wasn't a good idea.

His mind was finally matching up with his body—and his heart—when it came to Joel.

"Then let's be civilized and stuff our faces," Joel said. "And we'll see what happens after that."

Two slices each—one half pepperoni, the other half black olive and banana peppers, with onions over the whole thing—disappeared quickly enough that neither of them needed to break the silence.

Joel took a healthy swallow of his beer and sat back.

"I'm ready to answer your question. Got an answer for *me* yet?"

Duncan smiled. "Since you're a guest, it's only fair for you to go first. Then yes, I've got an answer."

Definitely not nearly as much truth as Joel was hoping for, of course, but Duncan would do the best he could with his carefully prepared backstory.

Same as he always did.

"Okay, about the laptop," Joel said, drumming the pads of his fingers on the table. "The problem is I don't really know what I want to do with what we find yet, and I probably *won't* know until we see what's there. Not exactly a master plan, I realize that. But I've never gotten into anything like this before, so I don't even know what our options are. I don't suppose it's the kind of thing you search for online."

"Not unless you're using a private browser. And over a clean connection at that. With a VPN, too."

Joel blew out through his lips and leaned forward.

"This is the kind of thing you just know off the top of your head? And you wonder why I asked whether *you've* done this before."

"It's no wonder you asked." Duncan flashed his best embarrassed smile. "I told you I worked with computers, and that I got burned out. What I didn't tell you is I spent time in cybersecurity. So yeah, I know my way around computer secrets, and how to protect them. Or not."

Joel narrowed his eyes, and Duncan wasn't surprised to see doubt there. He'd only talked in the most-vague terms about his previous jobs—always turning the subject back to his new job. Like most people, Joel had easily taken the bait of talking about himself.

But Duncan was afraid Joel'd been paying more attention than he let on the whole time.

"I didn't see that on your resume, or your application. You said network engineering and tech support. Are you trying to say your work was top secret or something like that?"

Duncan breathed in, held his breath, and slowly let it out, hoping he wasn't blowing strong pepperoni stink in Joel's face.

"It wasn't top secret, not in the way you're thinking. I could have listed what I did. Honestly, every time I've done that in the past, I end up getting dragged right back into the same line of work. And all the freaking horrible stress that goes with it. I didn't want any of that this time."

Once again, Duncan had told the truth. With only a little bit of careful spin.

Joel closed his eyes and rubbed his temples.

When he lowered his hands and looked back up, Duncan didn't see the disappointment or even anger he was worried about.

Joel seemed...impressed.

"So you lied?"

"Well, I hate to argue words, but I think *omitted* would be a more fair way to put it. I was in network engineering and tech support. Just a specialized area."

Joel tried to hide it, but a smile broke out for a quick second.

"Wow, you are splitting hairs there, aren't you? Am I wrong to guess someone who's not afraid to *omit* things from his resume won't worry too much about exploring an old abandoned laptop?"

Duncan's answering smile was lopsided, and genuine.

"You mean would you be corrupting me and leading me down a dark and dangerous path? Not a chance. If nothing else, this is an area where I know the lines and how to avoid crossing them. But if that path would be something new for *you*, you might want to take some time to consider how you feel about that."

Joel rolled his eyes, and his smile didn't disappear this time.

"Way ahead of you there, remember? Hell, I feel a lot better with someone who knows what he's doing. Otherwise I might stumble myself into real trouble. I'm game if you are, Duncan."

For a second, Duncan balanced on the edge of telling Joel everything.

About the now-absurd idea of spying on a damn parade float. How, while he certainly had a serious expertise in cybersecurity, he didn't exactly work *in* that field as much as he worked *around* it.

The way he'd gotten more suspicious about Bonnie Vincent and Grateful Grocer by the day, and decided he might want to drift back into his old line of work after all.

And *most* of all, Duncan wanted to tell Joel how much he thought the two of them might possibly have a damn good thing going.

If Joel didn't storm out after the first confession and never look back.

"Whenever you're ready," Duncan said.

Joel smacked his own thighs and got to his feet.

"Now seems like the perfect time to me. That way we can digest enough to go back for more pizza later. The only catch is this beast is so old I have to keep it plugged in. Here, or..."

Duncan shook his head.

"Easier to plug in from the couch. There's a power strip

under the coffee table. One of mine, so it's a good one. Want another beer? Or cider? Or something else?"

Joel was already on the way to the living room, laptop bag in hand.

"Sure, whatever you're having."

Duncan opened the fridge door, hesitated, then grabbed two cherry ciders. Cold, refreshing, and low-enough alcohol to keep them both clear-headed.

"Just shove some of those pillows out of the way," he said. "There are about a hundred too many in here."

Joel had the laptop plugged in and powering up, but he wiggled himself down into the every-possible-shade-of-tan pillows instead of tossing them overboard.

"I'm kinda digging this setup. Almost like getting buried at the beach without all the scratchy sand."

Duncan moved a few himself, just enough to land his backside on the bottom cushion, which was itself tan and remarkably overstuffed.

Not as close to Joel as he might have liked, but he could see the computer's screen just fine as it finally blinked into life.

Joel's fingers entered his password way too quick for Duncan to catch, not that he was normally *that* kind of spy.

"See, all the folders were there when I first booted up this creaky old thing," Joel said, tilting the screen toward Duncan. The tidy line of shortcuts looked a lot more like legal, HR, or accounting information than graphic design, with names like *Personnel*, *Investments*, and *Strategies*. "I had to add the links for my own stuff. Unless someone has changed the server addresses, they should all still work."

"That or the passwords. Mind if I suggest a few things before we dive right in?"

Joel shrugged, then handed the laptop over.

"Be my guest. Or I should say Grateful Grocer's guest, whether they know it or not."

"Making sure they *don't* know it is kind of the point."

He tapped the touchpad mouse with two fingers for a right click, then took a look at the properties of the shortcut named *Financials*.

"Set to read and write, and goes directly to the GG server. Assuming they haven't set up a new firewall or changed the password or drive mapping. You said you couldn't log in from the hotel, right?"

"Right, got a message about access forbidden or something like that. Then when I tried from home, the folder opened right up."

Duncan took a sip of his cider, giving himself time to consider. It hit exactly right after the pizza. Sharp and barely sweet, with only a slight boozy burn.

"So trying to hit it with a VPN connection probably won't work, and might get this machine blocked at long last. I'll take other precautions, but I'll need to work fast."

He glanced at Joel, who had his eyebrows raised.

"VPN is a new one on me."

"Sorry, that's virtual private network," Duncan said. "If I wander too far into jargon and acronym hell, please let me know. I don't want to be that kind of asshole."

Joel grinned, blue eyes twinkling.

"Don't worry, I'll let you know if you lapse into all the other varieties of asshole, too."

Duncan returned the smile, then went back to the computer.

Odds were uncomfortably high Joel would all too soon figure out how many nuances of asshole behavior Duncan had mastered over the years. For now, he wanted to enjoy the connection between them.

And pursue the secret in front of him.

He got to work.

21

Joel snuggled inside his grownup pillow fort, wishing he had the courage to shove them all aside and snuggle directly with Duncan instead.

Especially now, while he was intently focused on the dinosaur computer in his lap.

The pillows and sofa gave off a faint potpourri aroma that was too mild for Duncan to be the source, thank all the gods of good taste. Anyway, Duncan had more of a spicy, woodsy scent.

Joel couldn't help wondering if he'd chosen that deodorant or cologne or aftershave to remind him of something from his own past, or if he meant it to project something else altogether.

Duncan's background had always seemed a bit hazy, even after all the conversations they'd had.

Now it was downright mysterious.

And Joel couldn't pretend he didn't enjoy the possibilities shrouded in Duncan's history.

"We may be onto something here," Duncan said under his breath.

He'd clicked through several subfolders under *Financials* and opened a bunch of spreadsheets, then switched to another folder called *Cycles*.

"I never looked at that one," Joel said, leaning closer. "I thought it might be business cycles, which is a long way from my expertise."

Duncan breathed out through his nose in a soft snort, nothing like Joel's mortifying honks of laughter.

"Can't say it's too far away from mine. Damn, there's our first roadblock."

A box popped up on the screen, demanding a password.

"Does GG have a specific password protocol?" he went on. "Certain number of special characters, or changing it at a certain time?"

He turned to gaze into Joel's eyes from near enough to touch.

Or to kiss.

Joel blinked and shook his head to drag his brain back to the task at hand.

"They have... Yeah, they do. Eight characters, one number, one capital letter. There isn't any time limit on how often we have to change, though. At least not for me."

Duncan caught his lower lip between his teeth, and Joel hoped the warm flush he felt didn't show on his face.

"Okay, shouldn't be too hard to crack, but not from here.

I'd have to do that from the office, and probably from a computer with the right access. This one might do it given enough time. But I gotta say I'm already seeing plenty that looks suspicious, Joel. You want to hear more?"

Joel nodded at once.

"Isn't there a chance someone will know what we're doing with that computer? Even with whatever you did to sneak in? And didn't you just say you found something worth looking into?"

"I'd say what I've seen so far doesn't even scratch the surface."

"Then I'm already *in* whatever's going on, right? So tell me."

Duncan pulled up Excel and clicked through several open spreadsheets.

"You got it. Large sums in and out that don't make sense with that business cycle you mentioned, and that aren't documented very clearly. I'd be surprised if they don't match up with some of those big outlays you talked about for R&D or publicity. They're probably presented differently in the public accounts."

"So they're trying to cover their tracks, but not very well. Why wouldn't they use a password or something on those documents?"

"You'd be surprised how many people aren't as careful as they should be," Duncan said. "Anyway, this is a much older machine than yours, right? So it was possibly around at the beginning. Some of the file creation dates are close to ten years ago. Without looking at the system information or serial number, this computer might be in that neighborhood. Not to mention that password protocol you told me about is pretty outdated itself. Most places have much more strict guidelines these days."

Duncan turned sideways on the couch, one knee tucked onto the cushion, facing Joel.

"Listen, you met the contractor who gave you this. Think it's possible they grabbed a laptop that wasn't *meant* to be a loaner?"

Joel rubbed his face, nodding.

"I think it's likely. There were a couple of flustered contractors, and it was obvious even to me there should have been five or six more on the job. A whole bunch of people went to the same conference. I was added at the last minute as a new hire. Actually now that I think about it, the contractor said GG phased out loaners a while back, but I wasn't the only new person making the trip. So I got the worst of a bad bunch they had in storage."

Duncan's eyes went wide, and Joel couldn't help responding to the excitement he saw there.

Now the couch felt way too small, but he wasn't about to move.

"You're telling me they had a big expansion," Duncan said, "overworked contractors, new hires, and an out-of-town trip. And didn't you say the contractors were gone when you got back? I'd say the odds of lax security in a situation like that are higher than average. Especially when they seem to be spending a whole lot of money without a whole lot of thought about how to spend it."

"You mentioned the money moving in and out didn't make sense. Were there any big ones before all that expansion? Say around a year ago?"

Duncan laughed and leaned closer. Joel's breath caught when certain overly attentive parts of his body insisted a kiss was imminent.

"You're either naturally devious, or you know more about how criminals think than you give yourself credit for." Duncan clicked to one of the spreadsheets they'd been looking at before. "This one has been updated since you got hold of this machine. There was indeed a big amount going in not too long before that. What's even more interesting is a few big chunks went out around this time last year. Clearing the way, maybe."

Despite the amorous thoughts chasing around Joel's mind, curiosity shoved its way in.

"How about recently? For this blasted parade float, maybe?"

Duncan grinned, and he actually leaned toward Joel before he seemed to stop himself.

That didn't stop Joel's interior environment from heating up faster than the summertime air outside.

"Or hiring a much-needed assistant for you?" A few more taps. "There it is. Wow, this is...out of line no matter what they're expecting us to design."

Joel leaned closer this time, but to the laptop's dull-with-age screen.

"Please tell me I'm miscounting those zeros. Because that shows over three quarters of a million dollars."

Duncan shook his head.

"You got the right number of zeros, and that's one of the smallest numbers here."

Joel covered his mouth with one hand. His mind's active, curious corner had just taken what had to be an outrageous leap.

"What?" Duncan said. "Just say it."

"You said 'clearing the way' a minute ago, but I don't think you meant for headquarters expansion. Do you think they're doing something like laundering *money*, Duncan?"

Duncan sat back, and while his eyes were tight with what looked like worry, his broad smile said otherwise.

"That would be an *excellent* guess. I'm quite sure the amounts they got in before the expansion were substantially higher than what they spent. Maybe not traditional money laundering, since it sounds to me like they aren't exactly smart or careful about how they spend it, but I'd be surprised if it's not something along those lines." He stopped, watching Joel for several seconds. "What do you think...no, how do you *feel* about that?"

Joel opened his mouth to say...

He had no idea, so he closed it again.

Then he decided to let his currently mushy and convoluted thoughts attach themselves to words on the way out and damn the consequences.

"I understand we don't exactly have proof. But the main thing is I'm not even a little bit surprised, you know? A little shocked for sure. I mean, who takes a job expecting something like this to pop up less than a year later? Still..."

Duncan put the laptop on the coffee table, kicked off his shoes, and sat cross-legged on the couch, facing Joel."

"Still?"

Joel tapped one foot, not quite willing to slip his own shoes off and get quite that comfortable. This wasn't his place, for one thing, and Duncan hadn't suggested he should.

Even more, that would be too close to taking off other things and getting downright compromising.

"Still, I don't exactly feel bad about it. Not like I should protect the company or warn Ms. Vincent, or make an anonymous report to HR. When I think about the way she's acted toward me..."

He shook his head and kicked off his shoes after all, pushing a few pillows out of the way and imitating Duncan's cross-legged posture.

"And I don't have a bunch of close friends at work, but I know she's awful to other people as well. Hell, even if she was the nicest boss in the world, I don't want whatever this is brushed away and ignored. Does that make me an awful person?"

This time Duncan's lips curved slow and easy, and his eyes were more intense than worried.

"Not as far as I'm concerned. Do you think I'm an awful person for being willing to take your cues and dig into what you stumbled across?" His voice dropped and roughened. "Maybe doing a whole lot more than that?"

The warmth in Joel's middle seemed to compress itself into a pulsating sphere, then burst outward until it caressed every inch of his skin.

It wasn't Duncan's words, not exactly. It was more the way his voice changed, and the way his breathing wasn't faster, but deeper.

More powerful.

Like he was getting ready for something that didn't have a damn thing to do with computers or work or anything that existed outside the apartment.

Or outside the sofa, the few inches between their bodies.

Joel took a long, deep breath of his own.

"I wouldn't say you're *awful*, exactly. A little bit *devious* maybe." He shifted forward until their knees touched, and Duncan didn't move away. "And a whole hell of a lot *sexy* when you're hot on the trail of...something."

22

All of Duncan's reliable self-defense thoughts packed up and left him on his own, at the moment he'd needed them most in years.

He couldn't understand how Joel had regained the confidence—the *swagger*—he'd enjoyed the afternoon at the batting cage. Not when they were both sitting still, and when they were talking about zeros and ones and passwords and possible corporate crimes.

How could that possibly turn anyone on?

Anyone who hadn't done this kind of thing for a living for years, at least.

And yet Joel had moved closer, and the barest brush of contact between them carried a hell of a lot more force than knees touching through two layers of fabric had any right to.

Duncan felt the warmth of Joel's skin, caught his fresh, outdoorsy scent.

Barely caught himself before he fell headlong into Joel's bottomless blue eyes.

He knew the runaway beat of his heart came through in his voice, and he didn't care.

"I'm not...sure we should..."

Joel laughed deep in his chest, setting up a vibration that ricocheted through Duncan's whole body. He touched Duncan's hand, and the jolt of another connection made them both shiver.

"Probably not," Joel breathed. "I don't care."

And he moved closer, closing his eyes.

Some echo in the clamor of Duncan's mind insisted he should close his own eyes.

But he took in every detail of Joel's face in the endless instant before their lips met, wanting to remember the anticipation before the touch.

Light catching red highlights in Joel's brown hair. The fast pulse in the hollow of his throat. The spray of faint freckles across the bridge of his nose he'd never noticed before.

The pressure of Joel's tightening grip on Duncan's hand, the answering squeeze.

Then all that and everything else blasted away by their kiss.

Soft and gentle at first, barely more than a breath between them.

Intensifying as they both moved closer.

Lips parting, the taste of cider and a deeper sweetness.

Joel's strong arms around Duncan's waist, pulling them together.

Duncan gasped when Joel lifted him with what felt like no effort at all, turning their bodies until Duncan straddled Joel's lap.

Neither could mistake the hardness between them, straining to escape those two layers of fabric.

Warnings and alarm bells tried to grab hold of Duncan's mind without much success.

They barely knew each other, and Joel was technically Duncan's supervisor.

Work and play didn't mix. Especially when work in this case doubled up with two jobs.

One open, the other secret.

What finally broke through and cooled the flames enough for Duncan to draw back was knowing how much worse Joel would feel once the truth finally came out.

Because he couldn't imagine a way to avoid that horrible moment.

"Hang on." He leaned away, balancing himself with a grip on Joel's shoulders, trying to catch his breath. "This is too many kinds of bad idea, isn't it?"

Joel shook his head, eyes half-closed, his own breathing high and hot.

"Compared to *what?* Hacking into our employer's secure files?" He kissed Duncan's neck, first with his lips, then with tongue and teeth. "I say this is the best idea either of us have had for a long damn time."

When Joel shifted his attention to Duncan's earlobe, all Duncan managed was a groan.

His mind didn't reengage until Joel lifted him again,

stretching out on the couch with Duncan on top. The warmth of Joel's hands under his shirt got Duncan talking.

"This is... Damn it all to hell." Duncan shook his head and raised himself enough to look into Joel's eyes. "I can *not* believe I'm about to say this."

Now Joel's hands and the rest of him froze, and the desire in his eyes stilled.

But Duncan felt how fast their hearts beat together.

"If you're going to try to tell me we should wait or we're going too fast," Joel said, "I gotta say you're sending the worst mixed messages I've heard in my life."

"It's not that, gods no. There's nowhere I want to be more than right here, and no one else I want to be with." Duncan squeezed his eyes closed for a second. "But there's way too much you don't know about me, Joel. It would be shitty in the extreme for me to keep going without..."

Joel moved his hands away from Duncan's skin, and they both sat up.

Shirts on, no pants even unzipped. A reasonably safe distance between them.

But Duncan still felt cold where they'd touched.

And more exposed than if he'd been naked.

Joel scrubbed his hands through his already messy hair and shrugged.

"Okay then, Duncan. What's this big secret I need to know? Assuming there's only one, right?"

Duncan wanted to get up and pace, to give himself even more protection from the surging want still demanding satisfaction. But he'd made the mistake of letting himself get way too close to Joel for that.

Duncan's usual polite pushback and gentle disengagement speech wasn't going to work.

If he was as honest with himself as he wanted to be with Joel, disengagement was the last thing he wanted.

"Only one big secret." Duncan resumed his cross-legged posture, hoping to make it clear he wasn't running away. "I guess everything else falls under that one. I wasn't honest about why I started work at Grateful Grocer. I mean, I *have* enjoyed helping with the float and learning a little about graphics and all that, much more than I thought I would. And not only because of you."

Joel rolled his eyes and blew out through his lips, then rubbed his mouth. He sat facing the huge television, but turned enough that Duncan couldn't miss his scowl.

"Back to that fucking float that I wish I'd never heard one word about." Joel's voice rose as he spoke. "So what is it? Are you married, or involved with someone else? Are you more the illegal kind of hacker, on the run from the law? *What?*"

"Nothing like that. Nothing that...serious or reasonable, really. I heard about this gig while I was on a break from my regular work, that much is true. But I was hired to..."

Duncan was amazed and dismayed to have to fight back laughter of all blasted things. He was afraid he wouldn't be able to say something this absurd out loud no matter how much he wanted to.

Joel turned back toward him, waving one hand in a circle.

"Hired to what? Steal production secrets? Get ahead of

our R&D schedule? Or were you after the financials the whole damn time and my dumb ass happened to lead you right to it?"

Duncan caught Joel's hand, holding on when he tried to pull away.

"Joel, no. I wasn't after any of that. I tried to *keep* you from getting involved, remember?"

"But you were after *something*. Just say it, Duncan, and get it over with."

Duncan held his breath for a second, then squeezed Joel's hand.

"This might sound strange, but you got a lot closer than you think. I was hired to get the design for the float. That's all. I know how awful it sounds, I really do. I'm sorry."

Instead of staring open-mouthed at him like he'd just confessed to sneaking up behind Bonnie Vincent and goosing her, Joel's lips trembled and his eyes squeezed closed. He moved their hands as if he was shaking Duncan's, but sideways.

Then a snort not unlike both of them had struggled to fight back before erupted into the charged silence between them.

"The *float?*" Joel said, unable to hide his smile. "The fucking *float?* You've got to be kidding me. Who could possibly care enough about a stupid parade float to hire someone to *spy* on our design?"

But he didn't let go of Duncan's hand.

Duncan did his best, biting his lip and *ordering* his entire body to ignore the increasing urge to laugh. The internal mutiny continued instead. His stomach and chest twitched and his jaws ached from fighting a grin.

His eyes watering from suppressed mirth finally pushed him over the edge, and he and Joel collapsed toward each other in howls of laughter.

A few sputtered attempts at words followed, along with helpless clutching at each others' arms.

Joel finally got himself under control enough to speak between gasps, wiping tears from his cheeks the whole time.

"I had such a...a crazy list of things in my head. All the sins...you were about to...spring on me. But I never...*never*...expected what you actually said."

Duncan swiped his sleeve over his own face, waiting to let a giggle die down before he tried to talk.

"As bad as it sounded inside my head, and it sounded *terrible*, it was about a thousand times worse out in the air. How the hell did we get here?"

Joel took a huge breath, smiling while his shoulders rose and his chest and belly expanded. Another laugh snuck out when he exhaled.

"We got here because this whole region of Illinois is off the charts un*healthy* when it comes to the Rudolph County Harvest Festival and Parade, and Grateful Grocer and Bonnie Vincent successfully sucked me into their madness. But that doesn't quite let you off the hook for lying to me. No matter how stinking cute you are right now."

Duncan covered his hot eyes and face with his hands, shaking his head.

"I'm sorry," he said against his palms. "I truly am. I promise I'll tell you everything."

Then he bypassed his usual sensible hesitation so soon after a near-argument, dropped his hands, and leaned forward to drop a quick kiss on Joel's irresistible lips.

Thank all the deities of Finally Being Honest, Joel grabbed both of Duncan's hands instead of shoving him away.

"One thing you have to tell me, right now, before I'll consider anything else." Joel's gaze was so intense that Duncan only nodded. "Are you using a fake name?"

"No. Not on this job. I'm Duncan Edward Jackson through and through. And I'll still tell you the rest."

"Hell yes you will. Especially since we're embarking on a brand-new criminal enterprise together, and you're not even getting paid for that one, are you? Give me a minute to visit your restroom to compose *myself*, and get *yourself* ready to talk."

23

I t took longer in Duncan's equally over-cluttered restroom than Joel expected—staring into a mirror adorned with an obviously antique and swoopy gold-painted picture frame—but he eventually got himself settled down enough for company.

Duncan's company, to be exact, which he very much wanted to enjoy despite that unexpectedly bizarre confession.

Even after Duncan took his turn freshening up, the two of them agreed they required a few more slices of pizza and at least one more cider before they'd be ready for civilized conversation.

So Joel once again sat across from Duncan at the uber-kitschy little tiled table, stuffing his smile-achy face with pizza almost as good warm as it had been hot. With the odd little airy, happy aftereffects of a proper laughing fit still lingering in his chest and belly.

Wondering if he could possibly be considering getting involved with a freaking *spy* of all the other questionable boyfriend choices out in the world.

Well, the only question at this point was whether he should get *more* involved. Their lightning-hot couch tangle made it clear a few doors had already been blasted open.

"I think I'm suitably restored now," Duncan said as he pushed his chair back. "So let me get one question out of the way first thing and do my best with the others. I don't always know who hires me, because there's a go-between on a lot of jobs. Kind of like an agent or a broker. But on this one, I can tell you it was a big regional grocery store chain over toward St. Louis. Grateful Grocer is getting more attention than such a local chain should, not that either of us should be surprised by that now."

Joel was confused for a second, then he nodded with a grim smile.

"I'd heard rumors around town that a few entries into the parade got rejected because they didn't have any ties to Rudolph County. Easy enough to figure the rest out, not that I or anyone else is likely to care about the damn float in the end. How bizarre is it that I give a shit about GG when I'm willing to dig into their financial records with you?"

Duncan laughed, throaty and low and way too suggestively for Joel to ignore.

"After one of the strangest after-work nights I've had in my life? Not terribly bizarre."

Joel shook his head, then swallowed another mouthful of the crisp cider.

"I don't have enough information to be absolutely certain, but I'm gonna have to call bullshit on that one, Mr. Jackson. I'm willing to bet you've seen a lot more strange than you've admitted just yet. What exactly *is* the work you've had nights after?"

Duncan stared at Joel for several seconds without any of the closed-off look and feel he'd had before when the subject of his past came up. He shrugged and smiled.

"I suppose my cover is already blown to shreds and I still don't want to run, so why not? My regular work has been in corporate espionage since I finished college. Easy enough to call it spying, but without the cloak and dagger, or the really cool gadgets James Bond got from MI6. I mainly have a high-powered laptop and a near-impossible-to-trace cellphone for an internet uplink."

Joel blinked. And he'd thought the weirdest part was already behind them?

He let the first words to float to the wobbly surface of his mind continue out his mouth.

"*Near* impossible to trace? That's the best you or your employers could do?"

Duncan shrugged with one shoulder.

"My own personal superstition, though I've heard it around. If I don't say it *is* impossible, that makes me feel like I'm not tempting fate quite so much. Or temping technology is more like the truth."

"I feel the same way about...well, all kinds of things. Including new relationships, just so you know. And just how does one get into the corporate espionage business, Duncan?"

"I've heard about a bunch of different ways in that were much more interesting than mine." He crossed his legs and waved one hand in the air. "I really did expect to go into cybersecurity, and took a bunch of classes toward that. But I guess I got too ambitious trying to figure out what all I could hack into. You know, thinking I'd be able to catch the criminals if I discovered new and unique ways to commit their crimes before they did."

"Did you get caught?"

"Not by the authorities, though I was so clueless and careless I'm sure I eventually would have. One of my professors had been keeping her eye on me, using tools I didn't yet know existed to snoop network traffic and such. She called me in for a conference, which I thought meant I was either about to get kicked out on my ass or get extra credit for the semester. I'd recently found my way into our campus transit authority's scheduling and monitoring servers, and I'd been putting out feelers into the city's version."

Joel couldn't help laughing and leaning forward on his elbows.

"Were you going to shut something down? Or redirect buses the wrong way?"

"Nothing that bold. I honestly just wanted to see if I could. Anyway, she gave me a damn good scare to start with, which was the right thing to do. Then she told me I had other options besides cybersecurity if I was interested. She had classmates who'd gone into more than one kind of spy work, and offered to get me in touch with them."

Duncan grinned and laced his fingers together over his knee.

"Once I got over being freaking terrified, I was so excited I couldn't sit still. I tried to play it cool and failed miserably. From what I can recall, I basically blurted out something like 'Hell yes!' followed by 'Why aren't we talking to them right now?' The only reason I hadn't considered that line of work before was I didn't know where to start."

"But you were a natural." Joel couldn't keep the admiration out of his voice.

"Apparently. So, after talking with a few of her buddies, I turned down the idea of going under deep cover or infiltrating governments or sneaking behind enemy lines. Turns out I'm off the charts as far as typical curiosity goes, but too fond of myself to get into *that* kind of danger. The corporate world made sense. Less chance of a firing squad at dawn."

Joel couldn't stop his open-mouth smile and little gasp. As if he needed more reasons to be fascinated by Duncan.

"I remember you saying you were taking a break from a stressful job. True?"

Duncan raised his eyebrows and sighed, sounding like he'd just finished running a marathon.

"Painfully true. I had a longer-term gig than usual, and in a more stressful setting than I'd imagined. That's the hardest part, fitting in with people without getting too friendly and pretending to do the job because you *want* to. Yeah, that's the job description for me, but sometimes it gets to me more than normal. I'd planned to take six months off."

The chilly sensation of his heart sinking left Joel trying

not to shiver. He was sitting there with a *professional* pretender, and he'd do best to never forget that.

"I'm going to save one question and ask you a different one. Why'd you take the job at GG?"

"No surprise there, not really. Someone who gets into this line of work doesn't exactly thrive on relaxing and getting into a predictable routine. Seeking excitement ranks about as high as curiosity. Honestly, I was feeling...lethargic. Like I couldn't quite wake up no matter how much coffee I drank, or whether I went running or bike riding or anything else. I asked for an easy gig that might distract me long enough to get my mind sharp but not push me right back into stress."

The way Duncan's brow and mouth wrinkled made it clear he knew how that sounded, but Joel couldn't stop the words his churning gut pushed out.

"So which one is Grateful Grocery, and pretending to fit in with us ordinary folks? Distraction or stress?"

Duncan pulled out the chair next to Joel and moved over, never looking away from Joel's eyes. He took one of Joel's hands in both of his.

"Grateful Grocer in general? Especially Bonnie Vincent? That's a serious pain in the ass from start to finish." His lips twisted, and he looked down at their hands. "No, that's not really true. The job itself has been fun and a lot more interesting than I expected. But yeah, your boss is a solid piece of work. I'm not sure whether she thrives more on being stressed out or on making sure other people are."

Despite his discomfort, Joel couldn't help smiling.

"No arguments from me on any of that."

Duncan squeezed his hand, still looking down.

"Now *you*, on the other hand. You've been nothing but fascinating from the first second I saw you. I've never run across anyone who fills my needs for curiosity and excitement anywhere near as well as you do, Joel."

He finally looked up, and the cold in Joel's middle erupted into a firestorm at the lusty expression in his eyes.

"You literally get *paid* to lie," Joel said quietly. "To fit in, and make people trust you when they shouldn't. I haven't been the smartest guy in the world when it comes to relationships, but even I can see the warning signs with this one."

"No arguments from *me* on any of *that*. Even though I have to say I'm hardly James Bond in that department anyway. Depending on who I'm working for, the rules of engagement—or non-engagement in this case—are long and detailed and quite well communicated. This gig was a good bit more casual, but that doesn't mean my own rules don't apply. Should have applied, I should say. Getting romantically involved with anyone at the target site is near the top on anyone's Thou Shalt Not list. Including my own."

Duncan brushed Joel's palms light as a feather with his thumbs, sending shivers that violated at least one of those rules along Joel's arms and spine and straight between his legs.

"Yet here we are," Duncan whispered. "And all I want you to do is *stay* here."

Emboldened by that sizzling touch, Joel leaned forward enough to touch his lips to Duncan's. Barely an instant of contact, but somehow enough to drive the want lingering inside him back up to near boiling.

"Here we are. Even with all the warnings, I don't *want* to go."

Duncan dropped Joel's hand and reached up, both hands cupping Joel's face.

"Then don't."

His kiss and everything that came after easily convinced Joel the risk was worth it.

At least for the night.

Duncan normally slept soundly, no matter how difficult or challenging the current job. Once he was out of The Pretending Zone, some part of him relaxed enough to shut his mind down as soon as his head hit the pillow.

Especially after the kind of mind-obliterating sex he'd had with Joel. Not that he had much to compare the experience with, or even close.

He'd had plenty of opportunities over the years, and happily taken them.

But something about being with Joel took *Duncan* in a way he knew he wouldn't soon be able to forget.

And still, even with Joel curled close against his side, breathing softly, Duncan stared at the ceiling.

Toward the ceiling, anyway, since the first thing he'd done when he moved in was unplug what had to be every light-emitting sleep distraction ever invented. With the bright-green beam from the alarm clock, the piercing blue of the noise machine, multi-colored star and constellation projector, and foul-smelling scent diffuser (among others) defanged, he'd reduced the unwanted illumination a good bit. After yanking the several power strips required to drive all the other nonsense—and their brilliant red spotlights—the bedroom stayed tolerably dark.

All he needed after that was a quick raid of a hallway closet stuffed full of enough heavy comforters to stock a linen store showroom. Despite their overly cutesy but still earth-toned color schemes, the too-hot-for-summer things did a fine job of covering the filmy tan curtains that let in every shred of artificial light from outside long before the sun came up.

Joel stirred and grunted, turning so he faced Duncan without waking. The weight of one warm arm and leg across his body settled his nerves considerably, but not quite enough to calm his whirling mind.

Giving in to the lust brewing between him and Joel wasn't part of the trouble, at least not by itself. Letting his thoughts drift back a few hours to how damn well they fit together gave him a much-needed break from endless fretting, along with hoping Joel would be awake in time for a rematch before they had to leave for work.

Thoughts of the job itself spun everything back to uncomfortable.

On top of the aspiring-graphic-designer situation being fake even before he and Joel stumbled onto evidence of some kind of wrongdoing from the very top, now he had to add pretending this whole amazing night hadn't happened to the mix.

Then pretend to help Joel work on the ever-more-absurd parade float project, all while deciding what the hell to do about the very real possibility of money laundering or something like it.

Now throw in—on the off-chance that all of those things played out in a positive and survivable manner—digging in to what kind of relationship might be possible between them. If any kind was.

Duncan moved toward Joel, close enough to breathe in the scent of his tumbled and messy hair. Which, along with the rest of him, smelled about a million times better than anything the stink machine he'd unplugged could possibly offer.

Even with that, and easily the best sex he'd ever had, he still couldn't imagine how staying in very small and cozy Stidham, Illinois, might be a part of his future.

What he'd told Joel about the twin needs of curiosity and excitement that drove him were true. Joel promised to offer all of that and more when it came to a partner.

But small-town life, especially in only one small town, surely never could.

Duncan's job and lifestyle and personality had combined to give him a clearheaded understanding of his romantic life for the most part. He'd kept that balance well, with only a few longer-term exceptions.

Meet somebody not involved with his current gig, make sure they understood what he could give and what he couldn't, enjoy the time together, and move on with no one drowning in heartache and resentment. At least he hoped that had always been the case, and did his best to make sure of it.

But now?

The idea of moving on with the usual clean and tidy break made Duncan's heart feel like it was breaking into a thousand pieces, even with the man he didn't want to leave sleeping right beside him.

Duncan sank deeply enough into his preemptive regret that he twitched when Joel spoke.

"You okay?"

That deep, sleep-rough voice drove Duncan's worry away to the quietest corner of his mind. He kissed the top of Joel's head and took his chance to breathe in that sweet scent.

"Just thinking. I didn't mean to wake you."

Joel's head shook against his chest, and his hand stroked Duncan's side.

"Didn't wake me, not really. Noticed you weren't soft enough for sleep."

Duncan couldn't help giggling.

"Soft enough?"

Joel blew a slow, sleepy laugh across Duncan's chest, his cool breath raising a delightful ripple of goosebumps.

"Half asleep myself. Meant you felt too tense. Not quiet."

"That's *not* because you didn't relax me plenty, Joel. My mind gets wound up sometimes when I don't want it to. Go back to sleep."

Joel yawned and stretched, his muscles tensing and relaxing around Duncan's body.

"I will. You too. The world will still be there when you wake up."

He squeezed Duncan's ribs with his strong arm before leaning up enough to kiss his cheek. Joel's long, humming sigh did a lot to settle Duncan down all by itself.

Duncan let out his own sigh, instructing his agitated thoughts to exit his head at the same time.

None of this had to be decided right now, in the dark, in his warm bed.

Even if he did figure it all out, he couldn't do a damn thing about any of it until tomorrow.

Later today.

Whatever.

He turned onto his side, smiling when Joel and his incredibly comforting arm and leg followed.

Duncan held Joel's hand against his chest, and the one decision he could make was to enjoy where he was and let all the rest worry about itself.

25

Joel stood in Duncan's odd decades-old-sitcom throwback kitchen, breathing in the sharp, rich scent of fresh brewed coffee, and more or less staring into space.

Or into the glass-fronted cabinet full of way too many herbs, spices, and seasonings to be useful to anyone except a supermarket buyer, if that supermarket's customers demanded even more to choose from than Grateful Grocer offered.

No one needed seven kinds of salt, four varieties of paprika, and six kinds of dried thyme, did they? Not to mention several little bottles with writing he couldn't even read, or even hazard a guess at what the languages were. He wasn't quite motivated enough to get out his phone and try a translation app, but his busy, busy mind considered it.

He closed his eyes, sending the dizzying array of colors and labels out of his thoughts for the moment. A sip of the delicious brew helped. Much as he enjoyed the convenience of GG's coffee bombs, sometimes only fresh beans and water did the job.

The fancy copper-trimmed French press that had been tucked away in another cabinet produced a silky beverage that tasted like pure luxury going down.

Joel would need all the caffeine he could get to make it through what he hoped wasn't a terribly awkward day between himself and Duncan. Waking up two hours before he needed to—even with a quick trip home to change clothes—left his reserves a bit low.

He turned silently in his sock feet, looking into the living room and The Couch of Many Pillows. Sleep deprived or not, he couldn't help smiling at how many of those pillows were still scattered across the floor.

The pale light of sunrise was just bright enough to show that and the trail of discarded clothes he'd picked up on the way to the kitchen, putting his own on and stacking Duncan's on the coffee table.

Getting out of Duncan's warm bed had been the last thing he wanted to do, but a burst of antsy energy made the decision for him. The kind of jittery excitement that made staying still impossible even though it would drain away long before he could get back to sleep that night.

It would probably desert him sometime in the early after-noon, if memory served.

Joel had a lot to sort out before he tried to sleep, anyway. Before he went to work would be great, and with Duncan's participation would be best of all.

The rustle of comforter and sheets from the bedroom got Joel focused on the breakfast ingredients he had lined up and ready to go. No matter what happened today, he'd need enough food to absorb all the coffee he intended to drink.

The least he could do was make sure Duncan had the same.

He'd started the toast and had a huge batch of eggs stirred up and ready to scramble by the time he heard footsteps. The yolks were so deep-yellow the resulting froth was nearly orange.

He tried not to hold his breath, wondering what Duncan would say or do.

No matter how well two people got along the night before —and they'd gotten along unbelievably well—the morning after could be awkward as hell.

A warm hand on his shoulder got things off to a good start.

"Glad you're still here," Duncan said, and Joel could hear his smile. "When I woke up alone, I thought you might have fled in the night."

"Not before I had breakfast. Figured I'd make some for you while I'm at it."

Joel turned with his own smile and stepped into Duncan's arms, and for that moment, all the worries floated away like steam from his coffee.

"Smells great, but not as good as you do." Duncan spoke against Joel's ear before his lips moved along Joel's sensitive neck and shoulder.

"So I'm not the only one thinking I might need extra energy today?"

Joel caught Duncan's stubble-scratchy face in his hands, meeting his lips in a proper, freshly-brushed-teeth good morning kiss.

"After last night," Duncan said, "we're both going to need all the energy we can get. What can I do besides setting the table?"

With Duncan's choice of a pair of rather revealing denim shorts and a black t-shirt gone gray and butter-soft, Joel was tempted to tell him to forget breakfast and get his gorgeous ass right back into the bedroom.

"Grab whatever else you want to eat. I have the feeling it's going to be an interesting day."

Joel had cleared away the remains of their pizza party the night before, so he met Duncan at the cozy recycled-tile table and another set of mismatched plates. Fresh orange juice, applesauce, and a curvaceous yellow tomato so ripe it practically oozed summertime were welcome additions.

"I'm gonna bust out my advanced spy skills since that's not secret anymore," Duncan said with a wink, "and guess you didn't mean graphic design when you said today might get interesting."

Taking a minute to grab hold of his thoughts, Joel sprinkled his eggs with hot sauce and added a dollop of salsa.

"You *are* clever, especially for so early in the morning. As intriguing as our float design might get, I suspect my creaky old laptop will soak up all our attention. At work, anyway. All bets are off after that."

Joel jumped at Duncan's hand on his knee under the

table, then reached down to move Duncan's hand further up his leg.

"That's got to be the best thing I'll hear all day long," Duncan said, squeezing Joel's thigh before he let go. "Well, as your assistant, I'd say you can direct my work however you'd like. Even if it has nothing to do with the parade."

"Besides the obvious that's best done in private, you mean something like tracing unusual financial transactions? I'd guess you might need your own high-horsepower machine for that. It has to have better security than our pitiful abandoned loaner."

Duncan paused in slathering a generous amount of butter on his toast, one eyebrow raised and a smartass smile on his face.

"Oh yeah, *much* better security. I'll do my best to add a few barricades to your loaner, at least enough to keep it safe from prying eyes. It will never run the best of my tools that most people can't get their hands on, even if they know they exist. So we're both thinking dig in and see what we find, then decide what to do about it, huh?"

"Makes sense to me, but I'm not exactly experienced in the kind of underground work you do. Not that I'm not eager to learn more. Take that however you will."

"I'll take that as I'm glad we have plenty of time before we have to roll into GG headquarters, including time to shower before we go. As far as the right order of discovering and reporting, that really does depend. In this case, I'd suggest playing that by ear. If I find something alarming enough, I may call a halt and we decide who to talk to right then. Otherwise we can consider this a scouting expedition."

Joel sliced into the tomato, carving out two juicy rounds to drop onto his plate. One bite sent him into a closed-eyes groan. Sweet and tart and absolute perfection.

"Where did you *get* this? Even my grandparents didn't grow them this delicious."

Duncan grinned. "Don't you Grateful Grocer types know about the farmers market here in Stidham? Out where what has to be an old drive-in used to be. The best of the salad stuff came from there. Those eggs, too."

"No wonder everything is so good. I know Ms. Vincent is always trying to get local suppliers, but it looks like the best ones are holding out."

"I think you were right about some of the locals not being very happy with her, Joel. Not just the other grocery store owners, either. I heard a lot of chatter at the farmers market. It's amazing what people will say once they realize you're from out of town and assume you're a tourist."

Joel paused with the rest of the tomato slice halfway to his mouth.

"Were you looking for specific information when you went out there? Or just background research?"

"Just curious the first time. Then once I got suspicious about the boss, I went back to see what I could hear."

Nodding, Joel managed not to groan again even though the second bite of tomato was every bit as heavenly. As if trying to match the food-induced pleasure, Duncan took a sip of his coffee and sat back in his chair and sighed.

"*This* was in my apartment? Or did you sneak in some kind of top-secret blend?"

"That's your own coffee," Joel said. "I used the French press. Haven't you been using it?"

Duncan nearly spat out a second mouthful, but managed to swallow before laughing.

"I never even saw one in that overstuffed mess of a kitchen. I used an old drip machine, the first thing I dug out of a cabinet when I got here. Probably almost as old as your laptop. Now you know why I started getting my coffee at work instead."

"From the looks of this place, I'd bet we'd find a percolator from the Seventies if we looked for one. Probably a VCR and maybe a Betamax machine as well. We might even stumble across them while we're cleaning up from breakfast."

"I have a better idea." Duncan leaned toward Joel with a slow, seductive smile. "How about we finish breakfast first, then see what else we can get into before it's time to shower and head to work? Cleaning can wait. I say it's more important to build up a supply of pleasant memories to keep us going through what might turn into a rather odd day."

Joel couldn't help smiling back, and a tingle of heat started in his belly and worked its way up and down his body.

"No way I could possibly argue with such a logical, sensible idea. Not even if I wanted to."

Long before lunchtime, Duncan wished about a hundred times he could take back that prediction about his and Joel's day getting odd.

Not because his words successfully got Joel back into bed, thus proving to both of them that the night before hadn't been any kind of a fluke. Whatever sparked so hot and bright between them wasn't a one-time thing, and they were both glad to know it.

But *odd* didn't get anywhere near the atmosphere and attitudes at the Grateful Grocer headquarters that morning.

Duncan firmly resisted ideas about tempting fate or watching what he said for fear of speaking it into reality. Some of his family members could believe and live by that nonsense if it somehow made them feel better. Not him.

Except on days like this, when he struggled to keep from feeling responsible for everything uncomfortable.

He arrived about ten minutes after Joel, following their agreed-on plan to at least try to keep their relationship work-private, even if the *work* part might not last too much longer.

But before he got anywhere near Joel's secluded introvert-corner of an office, the silence in the normally chatty building felt like hot, itchy pressure against his skin.

Far more people were there than usual so early, for one thing.

And they were all much too quiet about it.

No good mornings, or cheery waves, or even smiles of greeting.

Everyone sat hunched over their computers, seeming to squeeze themselves as far away from the aisles and hallways as possible.

Even the low-level din of competing cubicle-music and radio was silent.

He couldn't say for sure, but he thought he smelled a whole lot more coffee on the air-conditioned breeze than he usually did before the afternoon caffeine rush.

Despite his twisting gut and clammy hands, Duncan kept his own morning smile in place and pretended not to notice when everyone refused to meet his eyes.

By the time he got to Joel's hideaway, Duncan was forcing himself to walk instead of breaking into a run. He'd never seen the door to Joel's office closed and it wasn't now, but he was mightily tempted to slam it and turn the lock.

He tried his best not to make too much noise, but Joel was on his feet and waving Duncan over at once.

"You're *finally* here," Joel whispered when Duncan got to

his desk. "I know it was my idea for us to get here at different times, but the last ten minutes felt like about a hundred years."

Duncan tucked his laptop bag out of sight under the desk and sat, unable to keep himself from glancing around for... something.

"What the hell's going on out there? I felt like I was about to walk into an instant trial with no chance for an appeal. With *my* neck headed straight for the guillotine."

Joel rolled his eyes and smiled, managing to look worried and sexy at the same time. His geeky shirt of the day was light blue with a burgundy pattern of anatomically correct hearts that you had get pleasantly close to see.

A nice inside joke between them, sure. As long as neither one of them ended up on the metaphorical firing line over their laptop escapades.

"Don't worry, they're not about to round us up and send us to the dungeon," Joel said. "At least not for the reasons you might be thinking. I can't imagine a group this dedicated to workplace gossip keeping anything that direct quiet. Anyway, the air of doom is too general to be focused on one department."

"Then what is it? Everyone's here so early, and none of them seem happy about it."

Joel shook his head.

"No idea yet. But everybody feels it. The break room is deserted. And even worse for GG, not a trace of the usual morning breakfast and snack temptations back there. First time that's happened since I started working here. To tell you the truth, there's usually *more* stuff out on the rare days someone leaves or gets fired."

"Sounds a lot like my family," Duncan said. "No better comfort than stuffing everyone's faces no matter how bad things get. I'm going to suggest we postpone our plans, then. Probably not the best idea to risk drawing attention to ourselves when the whole place is already on edge."

Joel raised his head and glanced at the door before he leaned closer to Duncan.

"Or, depending on what's going on, we might be better off doing it *now,* while people are distracted. Paying attention to keeping themselves quiet and out of sight, or too busy to look up. That could work to our advantage."

Joel's proud smile and his own inner swell of pride untwisted Duncan's nerves a tiny bit, but not without a quelling wash of guilt. He doubted Joel would have ever thought that way before the two of them crossed paths.

Now he'd mentally walked himself dangerously close to Duncan's own blurry morality when it came to information and all the sneaky ways to get it.

"That makes sense, but I still say we hold off until we have an idea of what's going on. Then we'll decide."

Joel stared at him for several long seconds, then grinned and nodded once.

"You got it." He touched his knee to Duncan's under the desk. "Glad to see you either way."

Before Duncan could work up his nerve to lean over for a risky kiss—which made him want it even more—someone rapped on the open door.

Rather than Bonnie Vincent and probably an even more extreme version of her typical manic mood, a quiet but worried looking Henry Koen stood there. Duncan realized he hadn't seen the GG building supervisor on his way through the food-photography-filled lobby or anywhere else, yet another oddity of the morning.

"Hey Henry," Joel said. "Come on in. Everything okay?"

Henry frowned and tilted his head to the side, his neat cap of silver curls glinting in the morning sunlight. He raised his big shoulders into an uneasy shrug for good measure.

"Can't say okay right now, but I'm hoping that's right around the corner. Just making the rounds to give folks the heads up. Wanted to make sure I didn't miss you two back here in your little hideaway."

He strolled inside and perched one hip on the edge of Joel's desk, looking intently at the corkboards covered with float design ideas. Something about the lively intelligence in that gaze gave Duncan no doubt he'd remember everything he saw.

Hell, Henry was the kind who might be able to accurately guess who'd submitted each and every idea he and Joel had picked out for more attention.

"Since you're both calm and happy," Henry said, "I'm gonna guess neither one of you stopped by one of our stores on the way in. Seems we had a major failure in the point-of-sale systems early this morning."

He paused, clearly waiting for a response Duncan couldn't deliver. Joel seemed every bit as confused.

"Point-of-sale systems?" Duncan said. "Neither one of us work on that side of things."

Henry waved one hand as if that wasn't a big deal. But he did glance over his shoulder toward the door.

"Consider yourself fortunate in that case. The POS systems pretty much run the stores. Inventory, checkout, pricing, the works. To the point that right now, not even the registers are working. The poor checkout kids can't even accept cash. Or they've been *told* they can't, because management here doesn't want the whole inventory system to go off the rails, which it will if there's no electronic or paper trail of the transactions."

Everything in Duncan's torso seemed to congeal into a knot. He and Joel hadn't gotten anywhere near that kind of software, but still.

"What could make a thing like that happen? If it's okay to ask."

"Sure, it's fine and dandy to ask," Henry said. "Especially since I'm not sure myself. Rumor is some part of the system wasn't installed properly during the big upgrade a few months back. Same time as we did so much expansion work on the building. You'll remember some of that, Joel. Anyway, the newest update busted it all to hell. To tell you the plain truth, I'm not too surprised about that, but I might be surprised the breakdown took this long."

Another glance over his shoulder, then Henry leaned closer.

"The reason I'm telling you two is Ms. Vincent is not exactly fit for company at the moment, but that's not stopping her from paying a visit to everyone in the building. From what I can tell, the ones working on solving the problem somehow got her to realize all her hovering and hellraising was keeping them from getting the whole operation back on a paying basis. So, she's turned more than her usual excess of energy and attention toward everyone else."

Duncan's internal organs resumed normal operations, and he and Joel exchanged a quick look.

"In other words," Joel said, "get busy, keep our heads down, and prepare for a sneak attack."

Henry's face broke into a smile that made him look about twenty years younger, and he smacked his own knee.

"That's about the measure of it. Probably best to stay in here as much as you can. The whole place is in panic mode, especially the poor folks in IT. Hope you don't have any kind of computer trouble today. Doubt you could get so much as a printer jam fixed or a password reset. Anyway, good luck."

He got up and headed toward the door.

"Thanks for the warning, Henry," Joel said.

Henry only raised one hand and kept going. Once he was out of sight, Duncan grabbed Joel's arm despite his earlier worries about someone seeing them.

"Remember what I said about spending a whole lot of money without much thought about how to spend it? I'm going to guess the expansion and hiring spree cost a fortune. But they never hired enough IT contractors, and sounds to me like the ones they hired weren't up to the job."

"They were at least focused on making a big splash where people could see it," Joel said. "And not thinking about the moving parts behind the scenes. That might explain why they're willing to pay me a ridiculous salary for marketing and ads with the best equipment for *my* job, but skimp on IT, who keep everything working."

Duncan moved away and winked.

"I'd say you're worth every penny and more." He rubbed his thighs, staring up at the ceiling, then glanced over his shoulder like Henry had. "Sounds like you were right about making our move while everyone is distracted, especially in IT. I doubt they have a spare second to watch unusual network activity when all the stores are dead in the water. What do you think?"

Joel blinked and opened his eyes wide, but his smile said he was more pleased than startled.

"I think that makes a lot of sense. And that we should jump before the mess gets straightened out. Let me pull up our preliminary designs onscreen so it won't look—"

A voice gone from unnaturally enthusiastic to downright arctic broke in.

"Hope you can tell me this one corner of our operations is functioning, boys. I'd sure like to think *someone* is getting work done today, so we won't be hemorrhaging cash from the whole damn corporation."

Joel tried to swallow, but his throat had transformed itself into a narrow tube made of nothing but sandpaper.

Too afraid to risk meeting Duncan's gaze, he turned toward the door.

Ms. Vincent stood there, hands jammed onto her hips, not bothering with her too-wide smile for a change. Instead her face was somehow *aggressively* blank, as if she wanted to be damn sure people knew how hard she was working to keep her anger and deep, deep disappointment from showing on the outside.

Even her clothes were out of character. He'd never seen her in anything as sedate and ordinary as a dark blue pantsuit and matching stacked heels, with a fluffy red blouse framing her neutral-angry expression.

Not a trace of a golf motif or anything flashy or trendy.

Maybe she'd been explaining the trouble to *her* higher-ups

already, the ones who might possibly be funneling cash through Grateful Grocer for reasons he and Duncan were hoping to dig up.

Or maybe she'd had difficult conversations with the store managers, who had to be frantic even so early in the morning. From Joel's limited early-morning shopping experience, people who were willing to get to the grocery store as soon as the doors opened weren't in the mood to waste time.

No wonder *her* mood wasn't exactly sunny.

The safest course had to be pretending he had no idea what might be going wrong all around them.

"Morning, Ms. Vincent," he managed with only a little bit of a rasp in his voice. "We were just opening up our design outlines to start really filling them in. Still looking like we'll be ready in plenty of time to start building the float."

The only sign of emotion she showed was lowering her head a tiny bit.

Not a good sign.

"You may find this hard to believe, Joel, but right now the parade is the last thing on my mind. Sorry to say it, but anything having to do with marketing and graphics and all the other things you boys do isn't anywhere near a priority for Grateful Grocer at the moment. We've got much more important things going on today. Or *not* going on, that's the hell of it. Things that really do pay the bills around here."

Joel's earlier bravado about how much he disliked this job —mainly because of the way the woman in front of him treated him—evaporated under her words. A surge of embarrassment and even shame flushed away all his ideas of getting out, or at the very least, getting even.

He couldn't even summon the courage to laugh to himself about knowing more about paying the bills at GG than Ms. Vincent would possibly believe. Or the strength in his voice or his arms and legs to do much of anything.

Duncan's sure and steady voice felt about a thousand miles away from what Joel could have managed.

"Sounds like we've got our work cut out for us more than ever, Ms. Vincent. Good thing we're making enough progress to be ahead of the game. Joel's got some fantastic ideas."

Ms. Vincent stared at Duncan, a faint frown tugging down the edges of her mouth.

He smiled back as if she'd just said how much she loved their draft layouts and couldn't wait to see the finished designs.

"I certainly hope so, boys," she said, shaking her head. "We've got a lot invested in this department. I'd sure hate to have to make changes and send those resources elsewhere."

She stood for several more seconds, not moving except slowly shifting her gaze between Joel and Duncan. Then she turned and strode out of the room.

"Looking for someone else to chew on, no doubt," Joel said, relieved to let his thoughts out without a leash. "Not sure whether she couldn't get a tooth in, or didn't like what she tasted."

Duncan turned to him with a wicked grin.

"I'm afraid you're getting cynical on me, young man. Probably long overdue from what I see around here today, but I'd hate to be responsible for such a stark change in your attitude."

Joel half-smiled. "Like hell you would. From what I see in *your* eyes right now, you couldn't be happier if the solution to our little mystery somehow landed right in your lap."

"Naaaah, where's the fun in that? Now if something else landed in my lap—or I should say some*one* else—that would be reason for celebrating. But I suppose we should put in a good day's work before pleasure."

"My line of work, the graphic design kind?" Joel winked. "Or your rather more secretive profession? And I'm all-in on the pleasure side, just for the record."

Duncan got to his feet, standing in front of the corkboards.

"I'll need your expertise to answer that one. Now that she's dropped by to patrol the waters, think she'll be back today? Or will she focus more of her joyful energy on the poor souls who're trying to fix the big problem?"

Joel got up and joined him, glad to be steady and strong on his feet now that Ms. Vincent was gone.

"She'll probably concentrate on the people she's most displeased by. But there hasn't been a problem this big since I've been working here, so it's possible she'll continue to roam the halls hunting for blood in the water."

"Then I think we should do enough now to create plausible cover," Duncan said. "Or you could play around with the designs while I sniff around for the files we're after. What do you think?"

"I'll send you two of the designs. Then you can have at least an image of them open on the old laptop in case someone drops by. It won't run Photoshop or InDesign or anything like that, but it should manage a simple PDF. And I'll work on the other two while you dig into the real project of the day. Not that I expect to ever finish any of the designs, or see them set free to roam the streets of downtown Stidham."

Duncan turned to him, a curious look in his eyes.

"Would you be terribly sad if your floats never broke through into reality?"

"*Our* floats, you mean. You'll get the credit or the blame on this as much as I will." Joel pushed his shoulder into Duncan's, wishing he could go in for a hug. "No, not terribly sad. They've got to pay me for the work whether I finish it or not. And if it weren't for this crazy parade, I never would have met you."

Without even checking over his shoulder, Duncan leaned in and gave Joel a quick peck on the cheek.

"I just hope you keep thinking that's a good thing once this whole adventure crosses the finish line."

28

The rest of the morning took on an oversaturated, hyperspeed distortion as soon as Duncan set up his powerhouse of a laptop and truly got to work.

He'd been calm to the point of actually enjoying himself when Bonnie Vincent pulled her ambush, and wanted to cheer when Joel didn't let himself get cowered or shamed into doing whatever it took to keep his crappy job.

He'd even taken himself off to the break room, *by* himself, to fetch coffee bombs to keep the two of them functioning.

Having a plan with decoy projects for cover made perfect sense on the surface, and the idea about everyone in IT being too distracted to pay attention today was logical. Especially when he added in how lax they'd been in tracking an errant laptop and random visits to network drives that should have been secured.

But he knew from more than enough experience that having the plan and executing it didn't always go as smoothly as expected.

The quiet, fearful atmosphere in the rest of the building hadn't dissipated at all. He felt sympathy for everyone trying their best to fix the trouble as early morning slipped into mid-morning, but he didn't mind the cover for his plans one bit.

No one else chatted or lingered in the break room, but the earthy, somehow desperate aroma of good old-fashioned drip coffeemakers in constant use made it clear someone had scurried in, and often. Seeking the comfort only watching boiling hot water seeping through ground beans to extract every bit of flavor could provide.

Perhaps because the sometimes-bitter undertaste fit the mood of the whole office.

Joel's grateful smile when Duncan delivered caffeine that was cold and smooth rather than overboiled and tasting of despair made the quick trip through The Land of Miserable Employees worth it.

"Thank you. I'm at that perfect stress balance point where coffee will keep me calmer instead of making me jittery. How's it looking out there?"

Duncan shook his head as he sat in front of the old beater laptop, already open with a float design on the screen.

"Not a word or even a glance from another human. And the air's so full of tension I feel like I need to scrub it off in a hot shower."

Duncan hadn't meant to sound flirtatious, but he welcomed Joel's naughty grin just the same.

"Once we get through this day, I can make that happen. Have I told you about the huge shower at my apartment? The one that's easily big enough for two?"

"You have not," Duncan said, giving Joel a naughty grin of his own. "Which, I might add, is a tragic omission. Sounds like I need to bring takeout to *your* place this evening. You ready?"

Joel's blue eyes sparkled, but his chest rose and fell in a long, slow breath.

"Let's do it. Something needs to change, so I might as well have a hand in it."

Duncan brought out his own laptop, which felt light and sleek as a black metallic feather compared to the pale-gray bulk of Joel's old croaker. He also retrieved one of the simplest workplace spying necessities ever repurposed from home decor and handed it to Joel.

"What's this for?" Joel turned the hexagonal mirror over in his hands. It was about as big as his palm, with the edges rounded and smooth. "Besides admiring myself in the less-than-flattering light around here."

"You have about the best lighting I've ever seen in an office. I've been meaning to ask how you managed that. It's a feng shui mirror, which works perfectly well for our purposes no matter how you feel about advantageous placement of furniture and such. Take the stand and angle it so you get a good view of the door."

Joel adjusted the wooden stand's position, looked over his shoulder, and nodded.

"That should catch my eye if anyone so much as pauses outside the door. Definitely if they stop or walk in. Do we need, I don't know..." He giggled and a most enchanting flush rose from his throat toward his face. "I was going to say a safe word, but that's not quite right."

A lovely tingling echo of the night before—and that same morning—rippled through Duncan's body, easing a bit of his own tension.

"A safe word can absolutely have its uses, so I'll file that pleasant idea away for later. For this, just my name will do. I'll keep another window on my laptop minimized so I can pop it up if I need to. How about a supplier for balloons or something like that?"

"Balloons it is. Now let's get to it before I finally lose my nerve."

Joel's eyebrows-raised grin didn't leave much room to think he'd lose his nerve for any reason at this point, but Duncan flipped open his own laptop and got to work.

He sent the float design projects to himself, opening one on each laptop. The one better fit for a doorstop than a computer took almost a minute to finally open the basic image.

His beast of a machine popped up the real design file he barely knew how to manipulate almost as soon as he double-clicked the icon.

With both minimized, he opened the folder shortcut on the desktop of the loaner, holding his breath while its creaky old brain trudged through its duties.

If someone had finally killed the unsecured access overnight, he and Joel would have a lot more work to get back in and snoop around.

Duncan's satisfied grunt when the files finally appeared got a quiet answer from Joel.

"Sounds like so far, so good."

"Looks like it. Now to see if I can't dig a little deeper."

He found the right cable in his bag, then linked the two machines. One of his favorite snooping programs connected and did its job in the time he needed to get a couple of good sips of his coffee.

Now his powerhouse laptop had a window showing the aged beast's desktop, including the open confidential files. More importantly, Duncan could drive the search with his own machine's greatly enhanced security to go with a lovely suite of investigative tools he couldn't wait to bring to the party.

Now that the job was before him, the worries and hesitation faded almost all the way to the background.

And he remembered for the first time in what felt like a lifetime why he loved his work in the first place.

Less than an hour later, he had no idea his thoughts were making it through to his mouth until Joel spoke.

"What did you say? It sounded a lot like *wow*."

Duncan blinked several times and shook his head, pulling his mind out of the hyperfocus that took him over at times like this.

"That's very much what I said." He paused everything, then closed his laptop out of long-standing habit before turning. "This place is a house of cards in a sandstorm, Joel. And I don't think Ms. Vincent is running the show at all, not when it comes to the side someone wants kept out of sight. But she sure as hell knows what's going on."

Joel rubbed his cheek with one hand while the beginnings of scowl showed on his face.

"If she's not in charge, who is?"

"None of that's in the files I've gotten to so far. But plenty of strange transfers are. Those spreadsheets and email accounts were password-protected, but not any kind of challenge to crack. I think..." Duncan scrubbed own his face before finishing the rest of his coffee.

"What it looks like to me is the whole setup is a front," he went on. "I doubt Grateful Grocer has ever come close to turning a profit going by their honest books, which are also on this server. And at the rate they're pouring cash into the operation with such low returns, they never will. But I honestly doubt they even want to."

"I can't believe it was all so easy to get to. Shouldn't stuff like this be a lot harder to uncover? This is like an open cash register while everyone's away at lunch."

Duncan laughed, glanced toward the open door, and rolled his chair closer to Joel.

"I don't know if I'd say it was *easy*. I might have hidden my skills and experience to get this gig, but this isn't exactly my first peek behind the curtains of a business. That, and I have a few tricks most folks can't just download off the internet."

"You know what I mean. I'm not dismissing your skills, or your tricks." Joel flashed a flirty smile. "Believe me, I know you're above average. I guess I'm surprised is all, even with the lucky break of some poor contractor giving me that laptop by accident."

Duncan patted the top of the laptop's screen.

"The mistake started before that. The hard drive should have been wiped clean or shredded before the laptop went into storage, or disposal, or whatever the first user actually meant to do with it. Assuming they meant to do anything, and this machine didn't get carried off by accident, or on purpose. If GG was getting rid of loaners altogether, I'd say any security protocol they had fell through the cracks. Bad for them, yeah. And good for anyone with an interest in how they operate behind the scenes."

Joel stared at the loaner laptop, currently running a sluggish screensaver made up of colorful lines unspooling against a black background.

"Do you have enough? To turn in, or report? However you usually handle something like this?"

Duncan shrugged. "When I've worked on something like this in the past, I had a specific objective in mind. A certain file, or pattern, or a communication string I was looking for. That was how I knew I was finished. Because I got what I was paid to dig up, and I knew exactly who to tell. In this case, it's more a question of getting the right authorities to listen. I don't know much about grocery store regulations and such, but financial regulators would be *very* interested in what we've got. You ready for that?"

Joel raised one eyebrow.

"What if I told you I wasn't? That I changed my mind about the whole thing. Would you still turn it in?"

Duncan puffed out a breath through his lips.

"I'm not sure you want my answer on that one, any more than I want to give it."

"I'm sure. Would that be any harder to do than telling me what you were actually here for? That couldn't have been easy to admit to."

Duncan laughed under his breath.

"Not really, and it only got worse once I started talking. Okay, you asked. At this point, with everything I've seen, yeah, I'd turn it all in. Anonymously, since no one higher up asked me to get involved. But there really is too much here to ignore."

Then to break the tension—in the air and growing too fast within himself—he couldn't help adding one more point.

"If you were asking about the float design, I haven't decided what to do about that yet. It all depends on whether you come up with a good one or not."

Duncan waited, watching Joel's eyes, not sure whether to hope for laughter, or even a smile.

He'd told the truth: adding yet another revelation to the pile Joel had already gotten out of him over the last couple of days.

Well, that wasn't really fair. He'd decided on his own to tell Joel. To clear the air between them, sure. And more than a little bit so Joel could make up his own mind about the situation between them before it went any further.

Like to bed.

Right now Joel only looked back, his whole face calm and neutral.

Duncan couldn't say the same for his mind, or his heart.

Instead of answering, Joel moved back, his face shifting to polite interest.

"Hi Ms. Vincent," he said. "Something I can help you with?"

29

Joel stared toward the open door, wondering if Duncan could hear his heart thudding inside his chest.

Ms. Vincent leaned against one side of the doorway, arms crossed, not giving a hint of how she felt or what she was thinking. Giving any sort of neutral emotional presentation wasn't the least bit like his usually overenthusiastic manager.

He had no idea how long she'd been there or what she'd heard.

Because he'd let himself get too caught up in Duncan's spy game after all, and stopped paying attention to anything else around them.

His mind showed no signs of helping now, either. It had snapped immediately from a heady mix of excitement and arousal to low-level panic.

He watched Duncan turn in what felt like slow motion, as if his chair moved a millimeter at a time.

At the rate Duncan moved, at least in Joel's mind, he'd finally be able to see Ms. Vincent lurking there sometime in January.

Joel already felt like his entire body had leaped seasons and frozen solid.

When she spoke, her voice was eerily calm and level.

"Hope I'm not interrupting anything important, boys. Everything's falling apart in about five different directions today, so it's hard to get anyone's attention. But I'm sure I don't have to remind either one of you that's how mistakes get made. When what we all know we *should* be focusing on what falls through the cracks."

Joel's low-level panic ratcheted itself up to red-alert level.

Duncan completed his turn in what now looked like lightning speed. And through some miracle of temperament, job experience, or maybe great sex that morning, *his* brain appeared to be functional, thank the gods.

"Sorry we didn't hear you trying to get our attention, Ms. Vincent. We were working on what we think is pretty important. The design for the parade float. If that's no longer the priority, I'm sure you'll let us know."

Joel looked over long enough to verify that Duncan was actually smiling to go along with that smooth, soothing voice, and he was amazed to see how easy and natural Duncan's face looked.

He turned back in time to see Ms. Vincent frown for a quick second before she got her chillingly calm face back on.

"That is what you were hired for, Duncan," she said. "To help Joel here get himself organized and get the job done. You boys definitely *look* busy with three laptops going at the same time. Got anything you need to show me, Joel? Or tell me about?"

Joel forced himself to hesitate, hoping to split the difference between seeming too eager to deny everything and too slow because he was desperately trying to think of what to say.

Which he was.

He decided to get as close to honest as he could, with a touch of redirection if he could manage it.

"You're welcome to check out the design boards, of course." He waved a trembling hand toward the four corkboards covered with images. "Our digital designs are kind of rough and in-progress so far, but feel free to take a look."

Ms. Vincent's sharp gaze took in the boards, but she didn't uncross her arms or step closer. At that distance, she'd probably see a colorful blur no matter how good her eyesight was.

Her suspicions—if they existed—clearly weren't going to be resolved by a detailed examination.

"I haven't had any reason to doubt your work so far. Or think either one of you wasn't giving us your best efforts." She nodded toward Duncan's end of the desk. "That's dedication for a new hire, Duncan, bringing in your own laptop and all. None of ours look quite that fancy. I suppose we really should think about getting you one that's up to the challenge. Assuming everything works out."

One side of her mouth curved in a tight smile that got nowhere near her eyes.

"I've still got a building full of fires to put out, so I'll let you boys get back to it."

Then she turned and walked away.

Joel dragged a breath in through what felt like iron bands around his chest before he dared to look at Duncan.

Who only returned Joel's look, still not seeming the least bit upset or off-balance.

"Just keep doing that, Joel. Breathing, I mean. From what I've seen around here, especially today, isn't it possible she's dropping by to visit everyone with the same not-quite-threats?"

"Possible? I guess it's possible, but do you really think she mentioned the damn laptops out of the blue for no reason at all?"

"Maybe she only noticed we had three, or that mine doesn't fit in, like she said. I think if she knew something was going on, she would have just walked in and taken the old one. Come on, don't panic just yet."

Joel shook his head and stared out the window. The day had started out overcast and stayed that way, leaving everything outside looking oddly one-dimensional and dull.

Kind of how he felt, which was jarring enough after the morning he'd had with Duncan to leave him sick to his stomach.

"I had every chance to stop, or to say no, didn't I? And the truth is as long as neither one of us actually ends up in jail or something like it, this is still the right thing to do. I just... I've never really gotten in trouble at work before, much less gotten fired. One of the benefits of contracting. Every job has had a predictable end date before now."

"I don't suppose I've ever gotten fired," Duncan said.

"Since most of the time I've been working for someone else behind the scenes. But I have been firmly asked to depart the premises a time or two. I learned to survive it. Especially since there's usually a very good reason I was there. Like you said, before now."

Joel's belly trembled, but not with its earlier upset. Now he was trying not to laugh, and that effort wasn't going well.

If Duncan was trying to distract him to make him feel better, it was working.

"You mean you don't think the Great Float Espionage Project is a good reason anymore?" A giggle escaped. "Hey, what are you going to do about that? Still planning to ruin GG's chances in the big parade?"

Duncan spun his chair, and by the time he came back around he was grinning.

"I haven't decided yet. If the people who sent me have it in for this place badly enough to want to steal a float design, they might give me a serious bonus for uncovering all the rest, you know? And I'd have to split that with you no matter what."

Joel's mirth faded, but his panic stayed away.

"That might not be a bad thing if I'm about to be out of a job without another one lined up. Maybe I should spend some time hunting one down just in case."

Duncan leaned forward and tapped one finger on the desk.

"That's something to consider whether any of this points back to you or not, you know. One of the tougher parts of my job is knowing exactly how bad shit is going to go when I'm on the way out the door, but I can't tell anyone I've been working with. There were times I didn't care, and times I really wanted to warn them. If things go really bad, the whole place might be out there looking with you."

Something tickled at the back of Joel's mind, but he couldn't quite grab it.

"I'd guess most people around here are as clueless as I was a few days ago, and I don't see how I can warn them. Not exactly a great way to make friends, I suppose. Not that I've made any tucked back here in my little introvert's kingdom. The only person I've really talked much to is…"

He squeezed his eyes closed, then forced himself to relax. Chasing a wayward thought never seemed to work.

But sometimes, pretending to ignore it could do the trick.

"Need more coffee?" Duncan said. "Or something to eat to soak up what you already had?"

"Just humor me for a minute. Think we really could rig up some way to run cold cases on our float? So we could hand out chilled stuff, like popsicles or soda, or even beer? Might even be able to convince marketing to coordinate the launch of the Coffee Bombs on the same day, and we could give those out iced."

Duncan's brow wrinkled in a confusion, but he smiled.

"I suppose so, if the budget truly is open. I'd guess you'd have to draw power from whatever makes the float go. That, or include a generator, which would probably be too noisy. Whoever handles the electrical stuff in the building should know who to ask, right?"

Joel's mind finally clicked into motion, and he grinned and squeezed Duncan's shoulder.

"That was exactly the push I needed. That would be Henry. He does a good bit of the electrical and maintenance work and supervises the rest, and I think *we* should talk to him again as soon as we can. He's been here since before GG took over this building, remember? He knows it inside and out. I'd lay odds he'll be here long after they're done no matter what we dig up. If anyone knows the secrets, or who might be behind the whole thing, it would be him."

"Maybe. He did say something about how he was surprised it took this long for a big problem to come up. The building expansion was squarely on that side of things, wasn't it? He would have noticed how much money got spent. I can probably figure out who the contractors were, but he'd know how they acted. If they thought anything was strange. What do you think, take him a coffee or something?"

"Nope, Henry's a tea man, believe it or not. Likes GG's English breakfast blend with his cream and sugar. I believe he's partial to Oreos with them to make things a little bit more unusual. I think he keeps a stash in the break room. Maybe we should pay him a visit since it's about midmorning snack time."

"Maybe *you* should," Duncan said. "He barely knows me except as your assistant."

Joel stood and stretched, aware of Duncan watching him and enjoying every second. That was a hell of a lot more pleasant than letting himself get more worried about what they were about to do.

"True, but that just means I'll start the conversation. You can pay close attention and ask the questions that make sense. The stuff I don't know to ask. Otherwise we'll spend the rest of the day with you pretending not to be irritated that I didn't get the information you wanted. And me pretending I'm not annoyed, because I *tried* to get you to come with me."

He pointed to one of the drawers under the desk that he'd never bothered using before now.

"If it helps, I'll lock your machines in there. I've had the key on my ring since I started here. Seems like a damn shame if I don't use it at least once."

Duncan looked doubtfully up at him, then locked both laptops and put them into the drawer. He got to his feet while Joel finally used his key, sadly without a sexy stretch of his own.

"You've got a point," Duncan said. "Let's fetch tea and Oreos and see what we can find out."

30

Rather than keeping his head up and his smile in place on the way back to the break room, Duncan paid a lot of attention to the soothing blue carpet.

If anything, the doom-laden mood in the building had gotten worse. Not like making his way through gummy cobwebs that clung to his skin anymore, bad as that was.

Now he felt like he and Joel were pushing through a thick layer of chilled, clammy gelatin that constantly threatened to spit them back out.

But that sour, soiled sensation was every bit as strong.

Everyone still quiet and trying to disappear into their desks, probably desperately trying to avoid catching Ms. Vincent's attention.

Once they finally made it to the break room, Duncan's head pounded with the strain. He turned to grab Joel's arm, possibly more, then froze.

The room wasn't as empty as he'd first thought.

Someone sat at a table near the wall of greenery, close enough to the window that Duncan couldn't tell who it was. Much like he and Joel had more than once to flirt and get to know each other.

Way back when Duncan thought this was going to be just another ordinary job, and a quick and easy one at that.

Before he could decide whether to stop or try to warn Joel, the mystery person raised one big hand.

Just the man they'd been looking for.

"Making it through the day so far?"

Joel waved back and headed that way.

"So far, Henry. Seemed like a good time to balance out all the caffeine with a little sugar."

Henry smiled and pointed to a neat row of little black cookies on one of Grateful Grocer's clever snack plates, this one shaped like an ear of corn. A steaming mug that looked like a luscious ripe tomato sat beside it.

"I think everyone in this place is at about triple-strength on everything today. Glad you're here. I was meaning to see if you had a minute to chat sometime today anyway. Seems like you two are the only ones who aren't too upset or scared to talk."

Duncan managed to keep from laughing out loud at that, but Joel gave him a don't-you-dare scowl anyway.

"I'll grab something for us," Duncan said. "Be right back."

"Got plenty of these cookies if you want," Henry said. "Just opened a fresh bag this morning."

Joel's smile instead of another glare made it clear Duncan

wasn't pushing too hard at all. They were both plenty eager to figure this whole thing out.

"Sounds great," Joel said. "They'll be just right with a couple of Coffee Bombs."

Duncan took the hint and grabbed the proper stimulants, pausing barely long enough to splash a little honey into both mugs because it was close by.

The idea of wasting possible honest-talking time with Henry when they could be interrupted at any minute had him more anxious than he wanted to admit.

Joel had somehow managed to fetch circular yellow plates shaped like cheery daisies while Duncan wasn't looking, and pile each high with Oreos.

"I don't want to take all your stash, Henry," Duncan said as he sat down with the coffee.

Henry waved both hands and grinned.

"Don't you worry about that. Doubt the two of you could out-cookie me when it comes to my all-time favorite. I got more put by than you'd think. More than my dear spouse knows about for sure. That's one secret I'd like very much to keep."

"I'd never tell a soul." Joel picked up one of the cream-filled black cookies and dunked it into his coffee, with no sign of his earlier nerves that Duncan could detect. "Everyone hanging in okay out there?"

Henry let out a long, gusty sigh as he dunked a cookie in his light brown tea.

"Far as I can tell, they're gonna have to call in a specialist from the company that programmed the point-of-sale system to clean it up. Some kind of problem with the servers here in the building."

He stared into Joel's eyes, then Duncan's.

"I can't say I know either one of you all that well, but after the years I've put in around here, I get a feeling about some folks. Seems to me you two know when to speak up and when to keep your mouths shut. Pay attention to what's going on around you at the same time. Sound about right?"

A churning heat altogether different from what Joel stirred up worked through Duncan's belly and chest. He didn't dare glance at Joel, but kept his eyes on Henry.

"I'd say so," Joel said. "I know Duncan's already been in more than one situation where his integrity came through loud and clear."

"I haven't been at Grateful Grocer too long," Duncan said, "but most of the jobs I've had involved knowing where the lines are. And how to avoid crossing them unless I have to."

Henry nodded as he bit off a softened bit of cookie, then chased it with a sip of tea.

"I thought as much. Well, it seems to me the servers weren't set up right in the first place. I'm no computer pro, but I'd say accusations like underpowered, not enough memory, and cabling not exactly right will be flying on those calls to the experts. The *expensive* experts. A whole lot of money got spent around here for failures this big to show up this soon."

"No wonder everyone's so tense," Joel said. "I'd hate to be in IT right now."

"You're not kidding," Henry said. "Most of them were hired new not long before you were. I spend a good bit of time back there, enough to make sure everything's at least cooled the way it should be. That's the one thing I can say was done right from the start, because *I* made sure of it. Anyway, I've heard several of our IT folks talk about jumping on board a slow-motion train wreck too late to stop it when it comes to taking this job."

Duncan didn't have to fake his shiver. He might not have the detailed knowledge an IT department had—or should have—but he'd been called in to root out the weaknesses often enough to get an idea of the nightmare in progress.

"All that and trying to keep the rest of the network up and running," he said. "Not to mention an angry manager breathing down their necks. I'd say they should be getting huge bonuses once this is all sorted out."

Henry snorted and waved another cookie in a circle over his teacup as if he was stirring the steam.

"Don't hold your breath on that one, even though I agree with you. The way I see it, they'll be getting the blame for all kinds of trouble they couldn't stop, and a bunch more they had nothing to do with starting. That train wreck I mentioned a minute ago? Those folks in IT will probably find themselves thrown under it no matter what they do. This bad day has been a long time coming, and I guess it won't be the last of a string of them."

Joel took a bite of his own dunked cookie and chased it with a sip of Coffee Bomb.

"Listen, I don't mean to sound like I don't trust you,

Henry, but why are you telling us all this? I'd hate for you to end up under that train yourself."

Henry smiled and shook his head slowly. Duncan couldn't help noticing how his bright eyes seemed to glow with the kind of sharp intelligence people might miss if they weren't paying attention.

An oversight that would be a mistake.

"Don't you worry about me, Joel," Henry said. "My contract isn't with Grateful Grocer at all. I'm an employee of the folks who own the building. Have been for years. Part of what they pay me for is keeping an eye on the businesses that lease the space. Keeping an eye on how steady their payments are likely to be, you might say. That's one thing any landlord doesn't much like, when a tenant up and breaks the lease and walks away, or doesn't give a warning when they're not going to renew. You're not the only one who's suspicious about what's been going on around here, Duncan."

Duncan sat back, a chilly jolt of fear pushing all the warmth away.

"I'm not sure I know what you mean," he said, trying to keep his voice reasonably steady.

"It's not like I'm gonna hustle off to Ms. Vincent or anyone else in management and turn you in," Henry said. "No reason why I'd do that with the way this place has been run lately. Truth is, if I was planning to do that, I would have a while back. Not long after you first started your work here."

Duncan looked at Joel, who only stared back with wide eyes and a pale face.

"Maybe you could say a little more about that," Joel said, turning back to Henry.

Henry took his time with the cookie and a sip of tea, then he nodded.

"Oh sure, glad to. See, one of the things I do is pay real close attention to folks who come to work here. Not just you, Duncan, but everyone. Take a quick peek into their backgrounds. You know, dig a little deeper than Grateful Grocer tends to do. You gave me a nice challenge, and I have to say thank you for that. Livened up my day quite a bit."

Duncan shrugged, deciding to find out as much as he could. If he was caught, he'd do himself a favor if he figured out how.

"Thank you, I guess? Mind telling me what you found?"

"Doubt it's anything you don't already know. What caught my attention was how much *didn't* seem to be there for one Mr. Duncan Jackson. Only took me a couple of minutes to uncover a whole bunch of aliases, see. But don't take that the wrong way. You had them set up just fine. Hardly anyone else would have noticed."

Duncan smiled and stared up at the ceiling.

"You're a private investigator aren't you, Henry? One of the perks of your job, and I'd bet one of the main responsibilities."

When he looked back, Henry held up an Oreo as if it were fine crystal. Duncan tapped it with his own in an odd spy-buddy toast.

"Figured you'd catch on pretty fast. Takes one to know one and all that."

Joel leaned forward, elbows on the table.

"Hang on. If you knew all this, why did you let them hire Duncan? Sounds to me like you're supposed to stop things like this."

31

Joel did his level best to act calmer than he felt, but doubted he was succeeding.

He felt like he was caught in some kind of frigid undercurrent that he'd never suspected could exist.

Neither Duncan nor Henry seemed the least bit upset about all they knew about each other. In fact, they were beaming at each other like long-lost brothers or some other such bullshit.

Meanwhile it was everything Joel could do to try to keep his head above water.

"I couldn't rightly call Duncan out for applying for a job under his real name," Henry said, frowning a little. "Not when I didn't see a thing besides that to worry about in his background. I did know to keep a close eye on what he might get into. Helping you seemed like a good thing to me, Joel, especially once everyone in this place started dumping a thousand-and-one ideas for this silly parade float onto your desk. I was afraid you'd disappear under all those piles."

Joel waved one hand, wishing he could use it to sort the jumble inside his head into some kind of order. Kind of like Duncan had done for his desk.

And maybe, possibly, hopefully, his love life.

"Okay, that makes sense," Joel said. "Is that all you saw, though?"

"Probably," Duncan said. "At first. Right?"

Henry twisted the top of his Oreo, neatly separating one black cookie from the white filling in the middle. He dunked the plain half, then popped it into his mouth.

"That's right. Until an odd computer name pinged through into the servers. One my security friends in IT couldn't find a record of for several months. Ring a bell for either of you?"

Joel stared down at his coffee, not trusting himself to look at either Henry or Duncan. He bit into one of his cookies without dunking, and his mouth enjoyed the sensation and taste as much as he had since he was a kid. The perfect balance of almost-burnt crunch with sweet, soft icing in the middle.

The rest of him was too preoccupied to notice such a simple pleasure.

"Rings a bell for me," Duncan said. "Why'd you let something like that go on if you knew about it?"

"Even after all my years keeping an eye on this place," Henry said, "I'm not the kind of cybersecurity expert you are. Grateful Grocer hasn't exactly made hiring one a priority, so neither is my IT buddy. I didn't have enough evidence to convince the building's owners to do anything, and hacking does cross the line when it comes to a leaseholder. But I knew from your background that you could run circles around me. So, I decided to let you do just that. I'd had the feeling something was pretty damn rotten for a while. Since the big building expansion, really. It was past time to figure out what."

Duncan looked at Joel and grinned.

"He gave us enough rope to tangle ourselves up with. Because it suited his own purposes. Have I got it about right?"

"Got it in one," Henry said, smiling. "I was planning to drop by before long and truly introduce myself, you might say, before you got in too deep. Enough to get yourself and a whole bunch more people into a real mess. But all the trouble today convinced me to speed up my timeline. From the looks of you two, I wasn't getting myself all stirred up over nothing."

"Nope," Duncan said. "I haven't had time to look at as much as I'd like to, but I saw more than enough that I'm sure the people behind Grateful Grocer would prefer to keep private. Along those lines, any chance this room could be less than private? Maybe a different kind of bug in all these plants?"

Henry chuckled and shook his head.

"Not a chance. Not in *my* building. It's the things I can't get hold of with my own two hands that we need to be worrying about."

"In that case, there's plenty to worry about," Duncan said.

"Of the financial kind, with a disturbing number of zeros attached."

"Wish I could say I was surprised," Henry said. "But you're doing a great job of confirming what I couldn't prove myself without maybe poking at a hornet nest because I didn't know any better. Not until now."

A chill prickled along Joel's spine.

"And that's why you warned us this morning, without really saying what you meant. Is that why Ms. Vincent stopped by again, talking about us having three laptops?"

Henry's white eyebrows went up, and he looked startled for the first time since Joel had known him.

Which only made Joel's own fears crank up several notches.

"Didn't know she'd done that. Tell me exactly what she said. Close as you can remember, anyway."

By the time he and Duncan recounted the conversation—and the sense of a planned ambush that went with it—Joel was further away than ever from believing it had been a random drop-in.

Henry rubbed the back of his neck while he stared down at his empty cookie plate.

"Well, I can't say I much like the sound of that. Were you still able to get into those files, Duncan? Or did you even get a chance to try?"

"The truth is both machines are safe in Joel's desk, and I locked them hard enough that anyone who managed to walk away with them would have a hell of a time getting into either one. I updated the security on that old machine just this morning. Then we came looking for you. You just happened to be here waiting for us."

"Isn't it nice when things work out like that?" Henry finished his tea, then tapped the side of his tomato mug with one finger. "Here's what I think, and I want to know how it strikes both of you before you do anything. I'd say make sure you can still get to those folders right quick. If you can, and if you believe you have enough to move forward, copy what you need to your own machine. Then get that machine out of here, however you need to do it."

Joel hadn't expected to say anything, but words tumbled out of his mouth.

"If your IT buddy knows to keep an eye on those files, does that mean they know what's in there? How bad it is? I guess I'm wondering if they could point Ms. Vincent or someone else right at Duncan."

Henry sat back and linked his fingers together over the soft round of his belly.

"You mean are the files easy to get *into* on top of being too easy to *find?* What do you say to that, Duncan? You're the expert."

Duncan shook his head, his gaze never leaving Joel's.

"Not unless they have the same kinds of tools I do, which they couldn't get just anywhere. Even if they did, they'd need a hell of a lot of practice using them."

He turned to Henry.

"That doesn't mean someone like Ms. Vincent or her higher-ups might not be paying more attention than I'd like.

But even she'd have a tough time opening them unless they're her files and she remembers the passwords. Didn't look like it to me with the way none of the file properties pointed back to her. Still, I'd say getting them copied as soon as I can is a good idea."

With Duncan and Henry watching him, obviously waiting for him to agree or not, Joel's mouth and throat and mind dried up as if he'd been eating cookies made of dust and sand. He gulped his coffee, which helped only enough to leave him clearing his throat before he tried to speak.

"Sounds like you two know what you're talking about when it comes to the private-eye side of things. Here's my idea. Duncan, I'd say it's high time we got in touch with some of the local vendors we might need for our float designs. How about you do that this afternoon so we'll know what's possible before we suggest something we can't get done—on any budget—to Ms. Vincent?"

Henry smiled and got to his feet, gathering up the cookie plates. Joel had somehow managed to eat several Oreos without noticing while they were talking. That or Duncan had grabbed them while he wasn't looking.

"Had a feeling we'd all get along once the time came," Henry said. "Now to figure out who to share all this scrumptious gossip with to keep the ball rolling. You two keep me posted and I'll do the same."

When he walked away, Duncan touched Joel's arm. His warm fingers on Joel's cold skin set up a chain reaction that seemed to go straight to his spine and spread out from there.

"That might mean you'll have to talk to Ms. Vincent alone if she pays a return visit. You good with that?"

Joel nudged Duncan's knee with his own under the table.

"I'm more okay with that than with her swooping in and catching you in the act. I do have a list of errands you can run, and some of them can actually be with vendors. As long as you report back with your progress—frequently—I think I'll be okay."

"Then that's what I'll do. I'll swing by my place first and take advantage of a great hiding place I found, not that I couldn't hide anything wherever I wanted to in all the stuff crammed in there. Next, I'll proceed right to your chore list, with plenty of check-ins along the way."

They both stood, and Joel tried not to let his imagination get too carried away with the break room as a safe space. One they'd regret leaving as soon as the Bad Stuff waiting for them really kicked in.

"Are you going to take both computers with you?" he said. "Or just yours?"

Duncan's fingers brushed against Joel's, but they didn't quite hold hands.

"Just mine. The old one does technically belong to GG whether they remember that or not. Want me to wipe out the shortcuts to those network drives before I go?"

"Yeah, go ahead. That way if she decides to sweat me, I won't be able to show her anything."

Duncan laughed and stopped at the doorway, right before they'd be chum in the highly distressed workplace water again.

"It's going to be okay, Joel. I won't be gone long. If something does go down, just send me a 911 text and I'll hustle my ass right back to your side."

32

Duncan did his best to hide it, but he was afraid Joel caught the anxiety gnawing around his edges before they fought their way through the sludgy office gloom and escaped to their introvert hideaway.

Joel's drawer was still closed, and Duncan didn't spot anything that had been moved or disturbed. Which didn't guarantee a thing, of course.

Still, it was better than the drawer sitting broken and empty, one or both machines missing, or anything else rifled through.

Joel was every bit as relieved, going by the way they both collapsed into their chairs with huge sighs. Duncan closed his eyes and pushed his chair into a slow rotation, not quite ready for pre-departure planning.

He wasn't thrilled about Henry catching him out so neatly, even though they seemed to have a hell of a lot in common. Most importantly, their shared certainty that things were rotten under Grateful Grocer's pristine and successful facade.

Leaving Joel alone when he was already nervous didn't sit especially well either. Not with the near certainty of Ms. Vincent dropping by for a return intimidation engagement.

Sure, Joel was a grown man who'd taken care of himself just fine before Duncan arrived.

But Duncan couldn't pretend he hadn't brought the reasons for Joel's current stress with him.

And leaving—at least for a while—couldn't be helped.

The necessity of getting his private machine and any evidence off-site was too obvious to ignore.

He wasn't alone in that concern, either.

"Okay, this should give you an excuse if you need one," Joel said.

Duncan brought his chair to a stop and opened his eyes, wishing he could give in to the urge to take a nap instead. Preferably snuggled up in bed with Joel, who held out a charmingly old-fashioned square of pale-green paper with *To Do* in heavy blue script across the top.

"An actual hand-written list in the age of the smartphone? I *adore* this."

Joel blushed and ducked his head, but he smiled.

"I know, I could have sent you a text message. One of my cousins got a big stack of these for the whole family a few years ago as a gag gift. And of course we all kept them, and use them, and we'll probably order more when they run out."

"I certainly hope so." Duncan scanned the list and

nodded. "Florist, balloon shop, print shop, burgers for lunch. Makes sense to me. Any of this a real priority, besides lunch?"

Joel covered his face with his hands and shook his head. When he looked up, he was still smiling but his eyes were tense and red.

"Not one single bit of it. Email or a phone call would do the job if that's what I was focused on. The only thing that really matters is what's *not* written down, and we can always order takeout. Do your real thing first and we'll go from there."

Duncan tucked the note into his pocket and leaned forward to meet Joel's gaze.

"I'll stay in touch, and you do the same. Just give me a few minutes to make sure we can still get in and to copy what I can. Work on your favorite design, maybe."

Joel rolled his eyes.

"Trying to distract me, which is a great idea. Yeah, let's both get moving. The sooner we do, the sooner this day will be over with. Hopefully we'll be celebrating instead of commiserating."

A ripple of unease caught Duncan by surprise at the idea of one versus the other. He generally only got hunches about his work when there was a trail he needed to follow, not when he was getting close to the goal.

And he rarely got them about anything personal, which might explain why he didn't have the best track record with relationships.

He couldn't shake the feeling of something unpleasant creeping up on him as he retrieved, unlocked, and fired up both laptops.

"Shortcuts still work," he said. "Copying now, but only a little at a time. Don't want to set off any network alarms at this point that might be too big to ignore, even with Henry involved and everything else going on."

Joel abandoned his pretense at work and scooted over to take a look. There wasn't much interesting to see besides the usual progress bar working its way from left to right.

"Do you encrypt the data or anything like that? Or back up to the cloud?"

Duncan dragged another batch of folders over.

"My whole machine is encrypted. Once I get everything, I'll use my phone to back it all up. Then when I have time and no rogue supervisors breathing down my neck, I can really dig in and see what's going on."

"Maybe we should kill that old laptop when you're finished," Joel said. "Nuke it somehow, but make it look like an accident. Or like it finally perished of old age. Then say that's why you brought your own in."

Duncan glanced at Joel with a quick wink.

"That's not a bad idea. It's already creaking and groaning pretty good. I haven't used a machine with a disk-based hard drive instead of solid-state for a long time."

The computer made a whirring sound that rose and fell, kind of like a ceiling fan that was badly out of balance. An occasional low *gronk* added to Duncan's recognition of an antique drive approaching the end of its life.

"I hate to admit I might not have paid it enough attention," Joel said. "But I think I would have noticed if it was making that much of a racket before."

Duncan switched folders and dragged over another batch, then tilted the laptop enough to touch the bottom of it.

"Running a little warm, but not too bad. I might be able to speed up its eventual demise if you want me to. Give it a heavy processing job to do, see if that helps. I'm not doing much with it right now, but it's struggling. Just about finished."

Joel glanced toward the door, causing Duncan's heart to wobble a bit in his chest. He managed to breathe again when Joel looked back with no signs of alarm.

"I'd say either that, or erase the whole thing," Joel said. "But I guess that might seem suspicious if anyone ever took a good look."

Duncan dragged the last batch of files onto his machine, tapping his foot with the nervous urge to get going.

"I'll wipe out those shortcuts from the old one's desktop and clean off the activity for the past couple of days. Then leave it running with those designs you sent me on the screen. If anyone happens to ask where my laptop went..."

"I'll say you needed it to show design demos. Hell, that's a perfect reason for you to bring yours today in the first place. Wish I'd thought of that earlier. Anyway, what a dedicated employee you are, Mr. Jackson."

"I'm learning from your excellent example, Mr. Cabot. Okay, that's got the old one cleared off, and my software deleted. I'll overwrite those parts of the drive with junk data to muddy things even more. Someone would have to be as good as me to follow my tracks from there."

Joel took a huge breath, held it, and blew out through his

lips, sending Duncan's dirty mind on a quick, pleasantly distracting trip.

"Then go, so you can get back here to me. And keep your phone on."

Duncan slipped his laptop back into its bag and stood. He very much wanted to see if a good, hard hug would relieve some of the tension in Joel's face and those strong shoulders, but that would be too risky for too many reasons.

If nothing else, if he himself was about to walk into a trap, the last thing he wanted was to drag Joel down with him.

"I'll probably drive you nuts checking in," Duncan said, "and I won't be gone long. But don't forget that 911 text if you need me, okay?"

Joel smiled and held up his phone.

"The one time tech is better than a paper to-do list. Hurry back."

Duncan took his own deep breath, slung the bag over his shoulder, and headed out before he could change his mind.

33

Joel watched Duncan walk away, forcing himself not to either go after him or call him back. And unable to keep himself from being a little disappointed when Duncan didn't stop.

He turned back to the design open on his screen that he didn't have a chance in hell of working on. No amount of staring or changing colors or moving objects around would make it anything more than a blur to his brain.

And if what Duncan and Henry were concerned about got brought into the open, odds were high no one at Grateful Grocer would give a damn about a parade float by the time October rolled around.

All those cookies sat like a sticky ball of lead in his belly, and the sugar hit on a mostly empty stomach made his head ache. Sadly, even if Kayleigh had been in the break room conjuring her magic treats, Joel didn't feel comfortable going back there.

Even the idea of walking through the gloom-heavy air got his guts twisting in sympathy with his stomach.

He took his phone out and set it on the desk where he could see it, something he rarely did at work. Not since he'd given up contracting and the constant need to be on the lookout for the next gig.

At least he hadn't been in a steady situation long enough to forget how to job hunt.

A flash of motion from Duncan's fancy mirror caught his attention, and Joel turned, hoping either Henry had dropped by to see how things were going or Duncan had returned to his senses and cut the faux errands short.

Rather than one of his hopes, the worst of his fears waited there instead.

Bonnie Vincent, hands on hips, chin raised, eyes flashing.

"Your assistant take an early afternoon off, Joel?"

Joel forced himself to pretend calm instead of grabbing for his phone and smashing that emergency text to Duncan.

"Hi, Ms. Vincent. He went out to run a couple of errands and grab lunch since Kayleigh's not here today. Need him to pick up anything for you?"

Ms. Vincent's thin, perfectly shaped eyebrows drew down.

"I'm the CEO of a grocery store chain. I believe I can manage to feed myself. Any reason he had to take his personal laptop with him to pick up lunch?"

Joel did his best to smile.

"He's going to show a few design demos to some of our potential suppliers before that. The spare I have can't run current software is all. If you need him to do something else instead, I can ask him to come back sooner."

"Duncan isn't *my* assistant last time I checked. He's *yours*. So no, *I* don't need him to do anything." She walked into Joel's office, stopping within touching distance of the croaker of a laptop. "If you're going to send him out on a lot of these *demos*, we'll find a computer for him. But I do hope he didn't take anything else with him, Joel. Something that belongs to Grateful Grocer, for example. He had to sign the same confidentiality agreements you did."

Joel could only hope the chilly sweat springing up all over his body didn't show through his clothes or on his face.

He should have sent that text to Duncan when he had the chance, because he could sure as hell use the backup.

But maybe he could borrow that confidence even without Duncan by his side.

"He has his own software, so that's not a worry. If we were supposed to keep the rough designs confidential, that's a mistake on my part, not his. I can get him back here in a few minutes. Or if there's some way we can help with the problems going on, please let me know."

He picked up his phone, not looking away from Ms. Vincent.

She flashed a cold smile.

"It's not the designs I'm worried about. And unless you plan to design special 'We're shut down system-wide so take your money to another grocery store' signs for us, I doubt you can do much to help on that side. *So* kind of you to offer."

She pointed at the old laptop.

"Any reason you need to keep this if Duncan's using his own now?"

Joel cleared his throat, wishing Duncan had taken the time to try to break the blasted thing on purpose.

But then he might not have gotten out with the data.

Assuming Ms. Vincent hadn't been waiting for him to leave before dropping by for another pleasant chat.

"No, go ahead and take it. I should have turned it in a while back, I know. But honestly, I forgot all about having it until Duncan needed one. I'm sorry about that."

Ms. Vincent picked up the laptop, shaking her head.

"Yes, you should have turned it in as soon as you got back from that conference. I'm finding out the hard way just how many mistakes were made a few months ago when it comes to IT. No one realizing you had this thing was one of them. I sure do hope I'm not about to discover a whole lot more."

She stared at him long enough that Joel was certain the nervous sweat showed on his face. If she kept it up, she'd see it start to trickle down his neck and spots show up all over his shirt.

"You don't have a clue the kind of pressure I'm under," she said. "Neither one of you or anyone else here does. Sloppy mistakes or laziness or simply not paying attention compounds every last bit of it. What I *don't* need is *any* employee deciding to go behind my back and try to solve problems that aren't any of their business in the first place."

All Joel could manage to do was nod.

"I didn't hire you or Duncan or anyone else to try to turn yourselves into some kind of power-to-the-worker heroes. And I don't suppose any of this is *your* problem in the end, is it? So you get back to your doodles and designs and I'll get back to keeping the damn company running."

Ms. Vincent watched Joel for another painfully long moment, then turned and walked out.

Joel sat forward with his elbows on his knees, forcing himself to breathe slowly. He didn't move until a couple of drops of sweat fell from his chin toward his shoes.

"Keep it together, Joel," he whispered. "Figure out what to do and do it. Don't you *dare* freeze up."

He leaned back and tried to unlock his phone, getting it done on the third try.

At this point, sending a text message seemed pointless. There was too much to say, for one thing.

Most of all, he wanted to hear Duncan's voice.

Thank the gods of good cellular signal and an attentive...

Boyfriend might be the right word after the night before, but damned if it didn't feel strange, even in his mind.

Either way, Duncan picked up right away.

"Is this a friendly check-in, or a vocal version of the 911 text?"

"We're definitely in emergency territory. Where are you?"

"Just stepping out of my apartment. Major damage, or more of a random visit?"

Joel used his sleeve to blot away some of the perspiration on his face.

"She took the old laptop with her. I wouldn't call it random at this point, not anymore."

"Got it. I'll get back there as soon as I can."

"Wait, Duncan, is that safe? Can they pick you up for stolen material or something like that? Or breaking the confidentiality agreement?"

Joel heard a door close in the background before Duncan answered.

"This isn't the time for it, but we'll have to have a talk about whistleblower protections at some point. I wouldn't have taken this gig in the first place—the parade float nonsense, I mean—if I wasn't pretty damn familiar with the law in Illinois. It's going to be okay."

Joel squeezed his eyes closed and shook his head, glad Duncan couldn't see him. Or hear how fast his heart was beating.

"Okay. Just get back here as soon as you can, then."

"I will. I promise."

Duncan leaned against the door in his apartment, eyes closed, heart beating faster than he expected.

This was nowhere near the first time he'd reached the get-in-touch-with-the-authorities stage of an investigation.

The timeline might have accelerated itself a bit, sure.

But that didn't explain his attack of the nerves.

That was down to getting himself involved with someone on the job, and the resulting worry about Joel.

He shook his head, opened his eyes, and went to an overly large corner cabinet beside the oven. One of the old ones that wasn't good for much, even with a jam-packed lazy Susan tucked inside.

Despite his reassurance to Joel—and despite knowing better—he'd shoved his laptop into the wasted space between a spinnable selection of every kind of grater and vegetable peeler and mortar-and-pestle ever sold during the 1990s. Even if an unbelievable string of events led to a search of this place, he doubted anyone would bother looking further after they spotted all that clutter.

Once he had the computer on the little tiled table and booted up, he stopped, tapping his fingers just under the keyboard.

The other grocery store chain would probably be tickled silly to get this news, but letting them have the information would only slow things down. Plus those same whistleblower laws he'd mentioned to Joel required him to report directly to a government agency, at least in Illinois.

Best to go straight to the top and get the ball rolling.

The hesitation itself showed how anxious he was. Normally he jumped right in and got the job done.

A couple of quick searches got him the contact information he needed, and his own credentials took care of the chance of long hold times.

Then after another few minutes of conversation, the data was on the way. Exactly what he'd planned to do after a little bit more digging.

What he hadn't planned for was the incredulous and eventually angry response on the other end of the line. Not at him or Joel, or anyone else working day-to-day for Grateful Grocer.

But the agent made it loud and clear the state's response was sure to be unusually quick and likely equally severe.

Duncan ended up feeling a little guilty he didn't have more to hand over to someone who was downright impatient to get the deeper investigation underway. Maybe what he'd given them would help the leads and suspicions they already had fit together.

And still, the truth was once the agents on the other end of the line took a look, they'd be able to dig a lot faster than he could. And with much bigger shovels.

He uploaded the data to his own secure storage before clearing it off his computer, more out of habit and a trace of professional paranoia than necessity. He wasn't about to let Bonnie Vincent or anyone else at Grateful Grocer get their hands on it, but taking stupid chances wasn't part of his spy game.

He'd just opened the cabinet door to stash the laptop when a message buzzed through on his phone.

Can't wait to see how your presentations went.

He groaned, irritated at almost making a big mistake after all. Why the hell would he ditch the machine when he was supposed to be out wooing suppliers?

Bag back over his shoulder and feeling like he'd been away for days instead of less than an hour, he sent a quick reply.

We'll get delivery and talk about it over lunch.

He stopped in the bathroom before leaving, determined not to look as rattled as he felt.

The last thing he wanted was to let a small-time operator like Ms. Vincent—or whoever was bankrolling the whole operation—throw him off-balance enough to cause a real problem.

He decided his flushed and sweaty face could make sense after being outside and putting on a sales pitch. Same with his ruffled hair. Even with the cloud cover, a warm breeze was bringing typical summertime temperatures back to Stidham, along with an extra-heavy dose of humidity.

The tense lines around his eyes and mouth had to go, though.

He forced his eyes shut. Forced his mouth into an exaggerated pucker, then opened wide. Forcing himself to breathe and relax made a difference, assuming he could keep the strain from creeping back in before he walked into work.

Blasting the silliest, happiest music he could find on the quick drive back at least gave him enough juice for a passable fake smile when he strolled past Henry's desk.

Henry looked up and nodded, his own face as friendly as ever.

"Good to see you, Duncan. Have a productive trip?"

"I think so. Got a lot done, but we'll have to wait to see how it all turns out."

Henry nodded and grinned.

"That often seems to be the way of it. Be sure and let me know if I can help."

"Will do."

Duncan sensed the same cowering silence in the office. If anything, people were a quick duck away from hiding under their desks. He barely paid attention to that. Nothing mattered except getting to Joel, and hopefully getting both of them out of there without a bunch of damage.

Everyone else at Grateful Grocer would have to fend for themselves.

Joel spun in his chair as soon as Duncan stepped into the office as if he'd coughed or dropped a bag full of glassware.

Joel's face was dead pale, and the sweat stains around his neck and armpits were obvious even from across the room.

"Sorry it took me so long," Duncan said. "A couple of the presentations went really well. I figure we'll hear something sooner than you think."

Joel rolled his eyes, and Duncan was convinced he was going to launch out of the chair for a hug.

One Duncan would have gladly returned under the circumstances.

"Somehow I knew you'd do a good job," Joel said. "Tell me how it went."

Duncan pulled his laptop out and put it on the desk before he sat, not wanting to invite questions about why he wasn't working. Then he leaned toward Joel, fighting the urge to hug him after all.

"You look wrung out. Has she been back?"

"I just hope I don't stink as bad as I feel. Haven't seen her since we talked, or heard anything. Did you get everything sent on its way?"

Duncan opened the laptop, wishing they'd had time to mock up some kind of presentation. He could walk out without risk to his career, but he didn't want Joel to worry about something dragging down his own future.

"All reported to the proper authorities. They couldn't tell me much, of course, but everyone I talked to sounded mighty interested. I got the feeling they'll move quick on this one, especially since I told them the target seems suspicious. You smell great to me, by the way."

Joel let out a breathy laugh and tugged at the middle of his shirt, lifting it away from his chest.

"Thanks, even though I know you're biased. Saying *target* sounds insane to me, but *suspicious* is right on the nose. She didn't much bother with subtlety. Said she hoped we understood about confidentiality agreements and how she didn't want a bunch of would-be heroes running around. Should we just call it a day and go home? Or pack up and make a run for the state line?"

Duncan closed his eyes for a second, letting his mind stray into the intensely pleasant memories he'd made with Joel back at his crammed-full apartment. The joys of a proper escape—with the two of them free to relax and be themselves and be anonymous at the same time—would have to wait.

"You have no idea how tempting that is to me right now. If I was the main guy instead of your assistant, I'd send you to my place to wait for me. But I guess we should at least tough it out until five. Didn't you mention getting take-out?"

This time Joel's laugh was real, and not as manic as Duncan feared.

"I don't know if I could eat, but we should definitely order. What are you in the mood for? When it comes to *food.*"

Duncan couldn't quite fight back a goofy giggle.

"You read my mind. I don't think I've ever admitted this to anyone, but this stage of a job absolutely gets me in the mood for a certain kind of distraction. And I already know you're damn good at taking my mind off things."

He leaned closer and took a breath. Nervous or not, Joel did smell downright amazing.

"As far as food, can we get those same cheeseburgers we had at the batting cage? To make up for me acting like a jerk because you were so fucking sexy in your shorts and t-shirt that I just about lost my mind along with my manners and good sense?"

Joel tried to fight his reaction, but the sexy flush rising from his shirt collar and climbing toward his face gave him away. A slow grin took over his worried face.

"I believe I can make that happen. As far as I know, they're on a different payment system than the stores, so that may be the only place in Illinois where GG can accept money."

"Not anymore," someone said from behind Duncan.

Joel's head jerked up, and the alarm in his eyes made Duncan's heart sink.

"Oh, hey Henry," Joel said with a relieved smile. "We were just thinking about ordering burgers from the batting cage. Did their systems go down too, or did the rest go back online?"

Duncan turned just as Henry strolled into the room, chuckling.

"That sounds mighty fine to me. I'd say they make the best burgers outside of my backyard grill. Gonna have to pass today, though. Got the feeling things are about to get pretty interesting around here. Want the good news, or the uncertain news?"

Joel stared at Duncan, eyes wide.

"How about both?" Duncan said.

Henry grunted, then went back and closed the office door.

No one spoke until he stopped beside Joel's desk.

"I'll go with the quick and easy first. Finally got the POS system back up and running. Just like I figured, a bunch of shortcuts they took during the upgrade and installation finally broke and brought everything else down with them."

"That's good news," Joel said, but his voice was shaky. "I suppose we should hear the rest while we're at it."

Henry nodded, and he didn't look anywhere near laughing now.

"Now that they've had a chance to catch their breath, I'm getting word from my friends in IT that something else is about to break. Sounds like this dam might take a whole lot more down when it goes. You do quick work, Duncan. Or whoever you got in touch with does."

In spite of his earlier confidence, Duncan didn't look at Joel.

Things were moving faster than he expected.

"I got the feeling they were surprised to have so much to go on," he said. "Or maybe what we had made the other pieces all fit. Think I need to get out sight?"

Joel kicked Duncan's ankle, not quite hard enough to hurt.

"You mean do *we* need to get out of sight."

Henry raised one eyebrow, but he didn't seem all that surprised by the display of team spirit.

"Not sure what to tell you there. I've been around here for a good long time, but never for something that might get this big, this fast." He stared out the window for a couple of seconds. "Now that I think about it, I might like a nice cheeseburger after all. Either one of you feel up to driving out there to pick them up? Might take both of you."

Joel stood so fast his chair scooted back across the carpet.

"I'm in, and I'll need Duncan's help for sure."

Duncan shook his head. "Pretty sure you can handle it by yourself. After all, I was already out of the office for a while today. I can take care of whatever happens here. I promise."

"I'm sure you could." Joel scowled down at him. "But I don't see any reason why you should have to. Sounds to me like things are already taking care of themselves. And we'll be easy to reach, right Henry? In case something comes up that we have to take care of."

"Got both your cell phone numbers. I know the line can get pretty long out there on a summer day, especially without the sun beating down. So go on now, and take your time."

35

Joel packed up as fast as he could, giving up on pretending to stay calm before he even started. Since he'd already sweated through his shirt, there wasn't much point in trying to hide.

"Should I do anything different with my computer?" he said. "It's not mine, so I guess I shouldn't take it. I'm just not sure whether we're trying for 'out to lunch' or more of a 'we're skipping town' kind of vibe."

Duncan already has his computer and everything else stowed and waiting.

"Aim for 'out to lunch.' We didn't turn in proprietary information like the research and development files or planned product launches or anything like that. And the truth is *you* didn't turn in a damn thing. Remember that."

"Would you cut that shit out? I'm not about to let you take

all the blowback for this. I'm the one who pushed you into going beyond the float business, remember?"

"I remember." Duncan stood with his bag over his shoulder and smiled. "I suppose you're a grown-ass man and can make your own decisions. You don't have much in the way of memorabilia or office clutter here anyway, so I'd say just leave our designs onscreen and call it done."

Joel glanced around, his chest aching as he realized no one would really notice if he did pack everything up and leave. The only things on his desk, now that the wave-about-to-crash pile of design suggestions was out of the way, were work-related.

No photos, no trinkets. No concert ticket stubs, no funny saying or song lyrics or poems hanging on the wall.

Just the damn corkboards covered with the best he and Duncan could scrounge out of the piles of stuff people basically threw at him.

Not because they thought he couldn't figure it out on his own, or that they all knew better.

Because they cared about something so strange and old-fashioned and seemingly unimportant as a holiday parade, and having the best float there.

They honestly wanted to help make it better, while he'd spent the whole time bitching and moaning to himself about how much they wanted to pitch in.

The place they cared about was about to go up in flames, or at least someone at the top was.

And Joel was halfway out the door, like he always had

been with all those contracting jobs. When all he'd wanted to do by taking this job was slow down and catch his breath.

He stopped and turned to Duncan.

"I'm not leaving."

Duncan scowled. "What? Don't put yourself through that, Joel. If the agencies really are moving fast enough for IT to notice, it could get pretty ugly around here. You don't want to be here for that kind of mess."

"That's not it. I played a pretty big part in whatever's coming, so I should see it through."

Duncan put his bag down and moved closer.

"You didn't do anything wrong. Hell, if I hadn't shown up, their secret would have stayed buried. Not forever, not with all the evidence they left and how deep a hole they dug, but it wouldn't have been today. None of this is your fault."

Joel smiled, reaching out to touch Duncan's arm.

"I know I didn't do anything wrong, and I'm *glad* you're here. I'm glad all of this happened. Not just because I think I'm falling in love with you, either."

Duncan blinked, and his mouth dropped open.

"I'm...glad to hear that," he said with a slow smile. "Not just because I'm falling in love with you, too. But I don't get why you want to hang around *here*."

"This place is rotten at the top, but that's not anyone's fault but the people *at* the top." Joel sat, waiting for Duncan to do the same. "I've been holding myself apart, like I'm superior or something. Like I decided to settle for this gig because I couldn't think of anything better to do. But the people here give a shit about this company, Duncan. They tried to welcome me, and they didn't even get upset when I wouldn't let them."

Duncan pursed his lips and leaned forward.

"Are you saying you want to drop the whole investigation? Because it's too late for that. Once I made that call, the secret was out."

"I know, and it should be. The only chance I see for this place to keep going is if they dig out the rot. The odds aren't great. I understand that. But it's a chance worth taking. I've been here for months, and I'd planned to stay for a lot longer. I doubt I'll stay forever, but I want to make that decision for myself. Don't you think it's about time I let myself give a shit too?"

Duncan tilted his head to one side and smiled.

"I guess I never thought about it that way. Not that I've ever stayed in one place long enough to even consider it. You sure you want to do it this way? I'll take all the heat. I've been here before. But it's still probably going to get hot enough to be uncomfortable for you."

Joel looked back at the designs they'd cobbled together, and at the stacks of contributions from his coworkers. He remembered how excited they'd all been bringing them in. Like kids bringing home their grade-school drawings for a proud parent to hang on the refrigerator.

"I'm sure. Pretty damn typical of me to decide I want to stay right when the whole thing starts to crumble. Maybe being brave enough to get to know you gave me the courage to figure the rest out. I've been leaning on other people's courage long enough."

Duncan was silent for a long while, then he frowned.

"Okay. Listen, if you're feeling like you want Grateful Grocer to weather this storm, then I'm a little worried what you might eventually think about me. About what I do. Pretty much everywhere else I've ever worked was full of people who cared about their jobs, and I was getting paid to upend all of that in some way. I know for damn sure a bunch of them don't have fond memories of me."

Joel waved his hand toward the building outside of his own cozy, introvert paradise of an office.

"From what you've told me, a bunch of those companies would have eventually imploded anyway, right? I mean, I can't promise folks here won't be upset once they realize what's going on. They might shove me out the door right after you. This way there's at least a chance things will work out for them. Otherwise Ms. Vincent and whoever's running this whole corrupt game would probably keep going until they really did burn the whole thing down."

He scooted closer to Duncan until their knees touched under the table.

"As far as how I feel about you, or how I'll feel in a week or a month or a year, I don't know how to answer that. Do you? I guess that's part of the whole falling in love thing. We don't know, but we take the chance anyway."

Duncan closed his eyes for a second and let out a breath.

"You're making too much sense all of a sudden. And you sound a whole lot less worried than I feel."

Joel laughed. "Really? I'm still scared half to death. My belly's tied up in a gummy Oreo knot and my heart's about to pound out of my chest. But I don't want to go anywhere, hopefully until it's on my own terms. Not because someone decided to take a good thing here and turn it into their own personal cash machine."

Duncan nudged Joel's knee and winked.

"Think you'll be able to live with my original plan to interfere with the Great Parade Float design?"

A gut-buster of a belly laugh Joel didn't think he had in him surprised both of them, and Joel quickly covered his mouth, hoping no one heard him out in the miserable Grateful Grocer world of people who had no idea what he could possibly find amusing today. He and Duncan managed to content themselves with an eye-watering fit of the giggles.

"About that," Joel said, wiping his cheeks. "I say we call that original gig collateral damage from whatever the state cooks up. Assuming there's a float at all, I think it should stay top secret."

Another giggle escaped Duncan, and he held out one hand.

"Deal. They may be disappointed when it comes to the parade, but I doubt they'll mind the overall outcome."

Joel shook the offered hand, holding on a good bit longer than necessary. That familiar thrilling spark went through him at Duncan's touch.

And the intensity of Duncan's gaze made it clear the feeling was entirely mutual.

"Well, Oreo belly or not," Joel said, "I'm getting too hungry to behave in a civilized manner. I'm going to order those cheeseburgers if you don't mind. Then we'll see what the rest of the day brings."

36

What the rest of the afternoon brought, from Duncan's perspective at least, turned out to be a whole lot of tense and seemingly endless waiting.

He and Joel devoured their lunches—kept perfectly warm in one of Grateful Grocer's thick, recycled-paper holders—and settled down to pretend to work.

Which consisted of an unsettled pattern of getting up to stare at the corkboards, pointing at one image or another, and pretending to discuss how they could incorporate the idea into the finished design. Then sitting down to at least look like they were busily making improvements to the graphics files.

Neither of them suggested taking turns glancing toward the door to make sure no one lurked there, but they naturally fell into the pattern anyway.

The frightened silence out in the rest of the building slowly lifted to the point that they heard people talking, cautiously quiet music, and even a couple of laughs. Nothing like a normal day for certain, but a huge improvement over the morning's crypt-like atmosphere.

The most Duncan could say for the time creeping by was he took the chance to dig in and get more familiar with the graphics software Joel seemed to use as easily as he breathed.

He doubted he'd ever feel totally comfortable with manipulating gradients and creating composite images, but he was definitely getting the hang of selecting parts of images and changing colors.

Joel had more of a settled, relaxed air about him than Duncan expected after the surprises of the morning. He'd shown a remarkable patience with having to repeat instructions over and over again that Duncan doubted he'd be able to match on a perfectly calm day.

But they never quite managed to lose the sense of being in the eye of the storm.

That storm finally broke when it was almost time to give up waiting and head out for the evening.

"Need one last coffee for the road?" Joel said, stretching with his arms over his head. "I'm too tired for this early, but the good thing is I doubt a little bit more caffeine would keep me from sleeping tonight. Eventually."

A warm, anticipatory tingle worked through Duncan's body, leaving him with no doubt that he'd be plenty awake for whatever Joel had planned. A nice caffeine boost would complement that anticipation quite nicely.

"I'd love one. Want me to brave the walk back to the break room to grab them so you don't have to?"

Joel looked at Duncan from under his eyebrows and batted his eyes.

"Why *ever* would I want you to do that? What could I possibly have to fear from my dear coworkers?"

Duncan snorted. "From your coworkers? Probably not a damn thing. That's not who I'm worried about."

"Then we'll brave the wilds together." Joel stood. "Might be nice to walk through while everyone's feeling so much better."

Before they could grab their mugs, Joel's office door slammed shut loud enough to make Duncan flinch.

The words that followed were frighteningly soft.

"Just where the hell do you think you're going?"

Ms. Vincent leaned against the door, arms crossed. She still wore her sensible pantsuit, but her hair was a rumpled mess and bright spots of color stood out on her cheeks.

Joel spoke before Duncan could grab the traffic jam of his thoughts. Turned out it was a whole lot easier to face a confrontation like this for himself, and *by* himself.

Having someone he cared about likely to get caught up in a blast of retribution—legal or not—threw him into an unexpected tailspin.

"Heading to the break room for coffee, Ms. Vincent," Joel said. "Need anything while we're back there?"

He sounded like he was talking to anyone else in the office. Maybe taking part in the great Midwestern tradition of discussing how the sun had finally clawed its way out to steam up the late afternoon.

"Just coffee, huh?" Ms. Vincent said, voice still quiet but

dripping with sarcasm. "I figured you were off to scoop up more documents. I hear it's hard to stop at just one when it comes to corporate theft."

"I'm not sure what you mean," Joel said. "We've been working on the float designs pretty much all day. You're welcome to take a look."

She walked toward them, shaking her head.

"Let's just pretend that's true, Joel. That you don't have a clue what's been going on right under your nose, which wouldn't be the claim of innocence you might think it is. How about you, Duncan? Anything on that fancy personal laptop I should be worried about?"

Remembering what Joel said about borrowing courage, Duncan raised his chin and faced her for himself.

"Not that I'm aware of. You can look at the designs with it, but they're easier to see on Joel's bigger screen."

Ms. Vincent took two quick steps closer and leaned forward, fists on the desk. It was everything Duncan could do to keep from scooting out of her range.

"You're going to look me in the eye and claim you haven't removed financial records from our servers? Then maybe you can explain why I'm getting nosy calls from state regulators, or exactly who you think has been snooping around in confidential files."

"I'm sorry. I can't help you with that," Duncan said. "I doubt someone in the graphics department would have access to those kinds of secured records. Maybe someone in IT can figure it out."

She lowered her head and took a long breath.

"Someone in IT *did* figure it out, even though they had more than enough to deal with today." She looked up at Duncan, eyes blazing. "Is that why you came here in the first place? To dig around where you don't belong and drag Joel down while you were at it?"

"Didn't you remind me earlier today that Duncan's *my* assistant, not yours?" Joel said. "That's why he's here, and he's damn good at it. I know you had a tough day today, everyone around here did. But that's no reason to accuse us or anyone else of stealing things."

Ms. Vincent thumped one fist on the table and shouted.

"We've got the laptop, Joel! We'll be able to *prove* who was digging through the files!"

Joel stepped around Duncan, pushing the chair back at the same time.

"That's enough. Neither one of us are going to put up with you yelling. You're going to have to handle whatever's going on, Ms. Vincent. Duncan and I will handle the doodles and designs."

He turned to Duncan, and now Joel's blue eyes burned hotter than the August sun outside.

"Seems to me we've done enough for one day. Time for us to wrap it up and get out of here."

Ms. Vincent stepped back, holding both hands up as if she were surrendering, but neither her furious expression nor her tight voice matched.

"Oh, I agree it's time for both of you to leave. *Past* damn time. You have no idea what you're wading into here, what kind of position you're putting *me* into. But that doesn't matter to *you*, does it?"

She turned and walked toward the door, stopping to look back over her shoulder before she opened it.

"Pack up all your crap and shut everything down. Your laptop stays here, Joel. Along with everything else you didn't bring in yourself. Duncan, do us both a favor and take yourself and your extra-special attitude and your goddamn laptop out of this building and out of my sight. And keep yourself there. You're both finished here as of right now."

She thew the door open hard enough to bounce it off the wall with a bang and left.

Duncan tried to control his breathing for a few seconds, then gave up and turned to Joel.

His cheeks were flushed and his breath heavy, but not as bad as Duncan's.

Joel winked and smiled.

"I think that went well, don't you?"

Duncan covered his mouth, but a most uncivilized honk of laughter escaped. He doubled over trying to contain it, not surprised to feel Joel's hand slapping his back as he failed to keep his own merriment under control.

"You are evil," Duncan managed to force out. "Evil and horrible and awful, and a terrible influence on me to top it all off."

Joel fell backward into his chair, again wiping away tears.

"Oh yeah, *I'm* the bad influence in this situation. Remind me again how *I* managed to get *you* into this mess?"

"You *absolutely* got me into this mess. That triple-damned laptop wasn't tucked away in *my* apartment, now was it?"

Joel shrugged and held up both hands.

"No argument, and no regrets. I guess we should get out of here while we've got the chance."

Duncan finally managed to catch his breath and grabbed Joel's arm.

"You know she can't do that, right? Those financial files went straight to the regulatory authorities and not anywhere else. Firing either one of us for doing that breaks yet another law in the great state of Illinois."

"Yeah, I know. I took a peek at those laws while you were out delivering your very effective sales pitches. On my phone, of course, because using a company computer for that kind of research would have been wrong. We'll get everything straightened out as much as we want to. Right now, what I want is to get you back to my place so we can relax. Maybe shower away the stress."

Duncan picked up his empty coffee mug and his laptop bag.

"Doubt I could take more caffeine at this point anyway. Should we let Henry know?"

Joel picked up his own bag and mug, then turned toward the door and grinned.

"I suspect Henry already knows."

Duncan turned just as a familiar voice spoke.

"Henry does indeed know," Henry said. "At least one pretty determined side of the story. Heard I need to collect your badges and escort you out of the building."

Joel waved him over.

"That's the plan," he said. "At least for now. Sorry to drag you into all of this when it's just about time to go home."

"You kidding me?" Henry said as he strolled into the office. "Going by what I hear from other departments, this mess has already grown to about the size of your average black hole, just keeping itself out of sight. Don't know what kind of pull you have there, Duncan, but I sure do hope to stay on your good side."

"Now I'm *sure* the agents already had the gears in motion and picking up speed before I got in touch," Duncan said. "Even with the hard information I had, they're moving unusually fast."

"So we might have stumbled on the missing piece to the puzzle." Joel's proud smile eased Duncan's worries about how all this turmoil would affect him. "What do you think, Henry? Time for us to lay low until the tide comes in?"

Henry slipped his hands into his pockets and nodded slowly.

"That's what I'd recommend, yep. Haven't seen anything quite like this in my years, but seems to me you two might enjoy a nice vacation for a few days. I've got all your contact information, so no worries about that. I'm gonna guess you know perfectly well you can't be fired for this, no matter what Ms. Vincent says."

Duncan grabbed his bag and waited for Joel to do the same. They each got out their employee badges.

"We do. Joel here tells me there's plenty to see and do

around this part of the state. I doubt I'll get bored anytime soon."

"He's right about that," Henry said as he took the badges. "Long as you can stand the heat. As far as the heat around here, I'll keep in touch. Think you can do the same, Duncan? If anything pops up that building management should know about?"

"Will do. I appreciate the professional courtesy, Henry."

Henry shook hands with both of them.

"I know you'll be fine," Joel said. "Especially if we keep out of sight for a bit. I don't want anyone taking things out on you. I hope most other folks around here are okay too."

Henry grinned.

"Folks seem to forget from time to time, but since I never worked for Grateful Grocer in the first place, I'm not going anywhere. You never can tell with situations like this, but I hope everything works out for the best for everyone. Including you, Joel. Come on then, let's get you started on that vacation."

37

The October morning of the Rudolph County Harvest Festival and Parade dawned cool and clear, with the nearly indigo sky promising sunshine for the big event.

In the parking lot behind the mellow brick of the Grateful Grocer headquarters building, a happily chatting group was busy putting the finishing touches on their much-anticipated parade float. All of them wore causal jeans and long-sleeved shirts appropriate for spending time at work on a Saturday. *Near* work at least, since they were outside enjoying the crisp air rather than inside under the office lights.

The float itself looked like a giant's version of well-stocked grocery shelves.

Huge three-dimensional versions of shiny apples and grapes of all colors. Brilliant carrots and eggplants and late summer squash. Mouth-watering breads and cakes. All lined up in front of pictures of perfectly cooked chicken, steak, and shrimp that looked almost real enough to smell.

No actual freezer cases lined the edges of the float, but big coolers were strategically hidden underneath all that massive food, tucked into images of specialty bowls and plates and kitchen gadgets not available anywhere else. Several warming boxes took up the rest of the space.

Inside waited samples of the best Grateful Grocer had to offer, especially Kayleigh's decadent treats.

Cookies and pastries, little bowls of autumnal soups and stewed fruits, cups of steaming apple cider, and ice cream.

All of it in GG-branded containers, with notes to "please bring the empties back to your local store for recycling for a special parade-attendee discount."

They even had little fruit- and veggie-shaped toys to hand out for kids and dogs alike.

Branded with the store logo, of course.

The new CEO had specifically asked Joel and Duncan if they wanted to help hand out the goodies along the parade route. She said it was the least the company could do to thank them for helping expose the criminal enterprise threatening to destroy what so many people had worked so hard to build.

After talking it over, they'd politely turned the offer down, saying they'd much rather help put the finishing touches on the float, then find a good spot to watch and cheer as it rolled by. It seemed only fair to let the newly reorganized company get itself out front and let bad associations from the past fade into memory.

Joel handed a box of Grateful Grocer's newest product to

a young man who knew exactly where to tuck it for easy retrieval.

Today was indeed the splashy debut of Coffee Bombs, including the unavoidable pumpkin spice flavor. The space right in front of the float held a playful, fall-colored illustration of how easy the brand-new product made caffeinated (or decaf) flavor delivery, along with a promise of tea and other indulgent beverages soon to come.

He'd never been a fan of the ubiquitous orange taste of October, but this compact and portable version wasn't half bad.

He turned just in time to see Duncan walk out of the big supply truck carrying another box of Coffee Bombs, this time cinnamon-and-ginger flavor.

The weather and change of wardrobe suited Duncan better than anything should have. He'd grown a neat black beard, and the rich golden color of his jacket brought out his gorgeous brown eyes and the warm tones of his skin.

Joel never would have considered himself a hopeless romantic only a few short months ago, but Duncan's grin still made him a little weak in the knees.

Hard to believe the thing he wanted most in the world had arrived in the form of a corporate spy pretending to be an assistant genuinely helping with the insane piles of work a seemingly simple parade float generated.

"Your big marketing triumph," Joel said. "I'm willing to bet Coffee Bombs will be the hit of the whole parade. They're already getting record orders across the whole chain."

Duncan handed the box up, then bumped Joel's shoulder with his.

"Across the *chains*, you mean. They're shipping these all over the Midwest. Just think how many people will be waking up with your groovy designs now."

Joel rolled his eyes, but his smile was real. The coffee beans interspersed with whatever the flavor was in the biodegradable wraps on each individual Bomb had turned out to be one of his favorite designs.

And probably one of his last, at least when it came to full-time work for Grateful Grocer.

He and Duncan headed back to the supply truck, which featured the GG logo along with the one from the much bigger multi-state chain it was now part of.

Turned out a couple of state agencies very much had their eyes on Ms. Vincent and her higher-ups for a good long while before Duncan got in touch. Their suspicions of falsified business records, underhanded accounting, and outright money laundering had been confirmed that day.

The result was swift and sharp for the group behind the swindle, and the threat to the whole company almost as serious. No trials yet, but no one doubted jail time loomed on the horizon.

Including for Ms. Vincent, who wouldn't be terrorizing anyone she considered beneath her anytime soon.

And thankfully the chain who'd hired Duncan to steal the parade design in the first place had gladly stepped in, bringing all the Grateful Grocer stores into the fold. They'd kept most of the amazing products and distributed them into all their original stores, with the GG name intact.

Joel had tried to fend off attention once his and Duncan's "vacation" ended and they went back to work, but word got out about what they'd done. After what seemed like a long stretch of cool glances and hurt feelings, everyone came around once the full story emerged.

Realizing how thick and nasty the rot at the top was, along with everyone who wasn't involved getting to keep their jobs, made all the difference. A few years of pay raise freezes to make up for sky-high salaries was offset by the great benefits package of the bigger chain.

All changes that had been too much on his and Duncan's minds over the last few days.

When he and Duncan got back to the truck, Henry Koen strolled toward them with a wave and a big grin. He still looked strange to Joel's eyes in faded jeans and an old St. Louis Cardinals sweatshirt instead of his work uniform.

"How you two holding up?" Henry clapped both of them on the back. "Looks plenty busy back here."

"We're good," Duncan said. "About ready to head out so we can get a good viewing spot. You riding on the float today?"

"No, not me. I figure all these kids who keep the stores up and running deserve that honor. Not to mention they'll hold up a lot better jumping off and back onto the float and handing things out than I would."

"I doubt that," Joel said. "I'd bet you're strong as a horse where it counts."

Henry waved that off, his silver curls sparkling in the sun.

"A true gentleman never lets all his strengths and weaknesses show. Given any more thought to what you're going to do now that this whole parade business is sorted out? I know they'd be real glad to see you stay, and I would too."

Joel looked at Duncan, and they shared a smile. That had been the subject of much discussion over the past week or so.

After a couple of months that had easily been the happiest of his life.

In the end, his unexpected choice had been far simpler than he expected.

"We're getting there," Joel said. "The truth is I'll be happy wherever Duncan is. I think he's just about made up his mind. Took him long enough."

Henry joined in their good-natured laughter, and Duncan bumped Joel's shoulder again.

The *real* truth was Joel couldn't imagine anyone who'd suit him better.

No matter where they ended up, he'd be fine as long as they were together.

Duncan tried to play it cool, but he was struck by the way the October sunlight caught in Joel's lovely blue eyes and brought out the reddish highlights in his hair.

Weeks sleeping beside Joel hadn't dimmed the simple pleasure of looking at him.

He doubted it ever would.

Especially when Joel wore jeans that hugged his strong legs and backside, and a lumberjack-adjacent red-and-blue flannel shirt that emphasized those broad shoulders.

A guy could get hooked on waking up beside someone that hot and handsome.

Luckily for Duncan, Joel felt the same way. And moving out of his hectic 90s museum apartment and into Joel's far more harmonious place only turned up their attraction while deepening their friendship.

"Well, I offered to settle here as a home base," he said,

answering Henry's question. "You know, head out on my day job adventures and get myself back here as often as I could. But I think Joel's been craving my nomadic lifestyle. At least for a while."

"That's the thing about graphic design work." Joel's blush and shy smile set Duncan to daydreaming about what they'd get up to that afternoon and evening. "As long as I've got a computer and an internet connection, I can work from anywhere in the world."

Henry's eyebrows went up.

"World-wide, huh? That's quite a step up from working in small-town Southern Illinois."

It was Duncan's turn to wave the idea away.

"I'm not sure about that part, but you never know. There's plenty of work stateside as long as people keep making questionable business choices. Which you know they will. I get the feeling I'll be a whole lot happier coming home to something besides a lonely hotel room or rental after a stressful day of pretending to fit in."

"I'll still be able to do contract work for Grateful Grocer," Joel said. "And I'd like to do that as long as they need me. With the merger, they really don't need me full-time anymore."

"They may not need you," Henry said, "but they're damn lucky you're willing to stay involved. You do fine work, Joel, and you did a fine job training your assistant here."

Duncan looked at the float, amazed all over again at the fantastic job Joel had done with the design, and everyone else had done bringing it to life. He'd enjoyed his support role immensely, from contacting vendors to looking at prototypes to fine-tuning the end results.

He understood why the now-parent grocery store chain had been so eager to steal the design, which he'd refused to share until the very end. And he doubted they would have created anything anywhere near as spectacular even if they'd had every detail in advance.

Not without Joel's brilliant vision driving the whole thing.

Joel was the spark in more ways than one.

"I'm hardly at his level when it comes to design," Duncan said, "and I never will be. But I know a whole lot more about graphics than I did when I started. And grocery stores. Joel's come a long way when it comes to the finer side of IT and all kinds of other technology, too."

Henry nodded, with a mischievous grin that made him look about twenty years old.

"That's two mighty fine sets of skills to have. When do you think you might head out of town?"

"That all depends on when Duncan's next assignment comes through," Joel said. "I don't have a lot to pack at my apartment, so that part will be easy. We still need to visit his place in Chicago. Might make a nice home base for a while with the big airports and train station and all."

The thought of being with Joel in his own apartment, on his home turf, delighted Duncan to no end. He'd even gotten a little homesick for the rhythms of the big city and the lake since the miserable summer heat broke. Autumn in Chicago was a delight he couldn't wait to share.

"You'll always be welcome for a visit," Duncan said. "Or

to stay, even if we're not in town. You and your wife both. If we're home, we'll take you out on the town in return for all your help when the dam broke around here, and for having us over for dinner so many times."

"Cindy and I might just take you up on that," Henry said. "She's got a birthday coming up, and a big trip would do us both good. It's been too long. Either way, I hope to hear from you once in a while. No matter how you got started, you did a good thing and gave this company a chance to survive. It's been fine knowing both of you."

"You too, Henry," Joel said. "I don't know how I would have gotten through all the uproar without you."

"Sure you do." Henry patted Duncan's shoulder. "You two have each other. That makes up for a whole lot."

Duncan looked at Joel again, then took his hand. The warmth of that contact made its way through Duncan's whole body in one joyful beat of his heart.

All his strict rules about never getting involved with anyone at work had made perfect sense for years, and he'd tell anyone newly getting into the spy game to follow his example.

But he knew now that his wall of protection had collapsed the first time he looked into Joel's eyes.

He'd never been more grateful for breaking his own rules in his life.

Especially since that break had transformed his life in a thousand ways, with more promised on the horizon.

All of them for the best.

"Knowing Joel certainly makes up for a whole lot for me.

Coming to Stidham turned out to be the best decision I've made in a long, long time."

He took Joel's hand, bumping his shoulder again.

"Maybe my best one ever."

Thank you for joining Duncan and Joel
on their path to Happily Ever After!

For more romance from Kari Kilgore, turn the page
or visit www.KariKilgore.com/Romance.

ALSO BY KARI KILGORE

I hope you enjoyed reading *The Coffee Bomb and the Corporate Spy* as much as I enjoyed writing it.

If you're in the mood for more romance, swing by www.KariKilgore.com/Romance.

For more tales with LGBTQ+ characters in almost every genre, head over to www.KariKilgore.com/LGBTQStories.

Be the first to know about release dates and check out more of my fiction, including almost every genre with plenty of romantic elements, at www.KariKilgore.com.

Romance:

Protecting Her Own

The Box of Possibilities

Escape into Romance: A Collection of Sweet Beginnings

Partners in Romance with Jason A. Adams:

Stories with Strong Romantic Elements:

The Voices through Time Series:

Songs in the Mountain

Secrets in the Land

Sorrows in the Earth

Walking the Ghosts: A Voices through Time Novella

The Odd Society:

Independent by Means of Magic

Protected by Means of Magic

The Storms of Future Past Series:

Dreaming the Storm

Joining the Storm

Into the Storm

Fighting the Storm

Sensing the Storm: A Storms of Future Past Prequel

Storms of the Heart: A Storms of Future Past Romance

Storms of Future Past Books One through Four Collection

Investigations Beyond Belief: The Initial Adventures of Deb Powers: Otherworldly PI

A Tapestry of Holiday Tales: Winter Adventures from the Odds and Endings Bookstore

Novels:

Until Death

The Dream Thief

Hand Me Downs

The Great Gold Record Heist

Novellas:

Legacy of the Land

In the Pines

DNA Never Lies

Murder at the Fabulous Feline Emporium

Team Building Revenge

Dispatches from the Galaxy Stories:

Restricted Species

The Becalmed

The Garbage Belt

Plurapod Pathogen

The Changes Cascade

Collections:

Fantastic Women: A Dark Fantasy Novella Trio

Fantastic Shorts: Volume 1

Fantastic Shorts: Volume 2

Fantastic Shorts: Volume 3

Stepping Out of Reality: Short Spells of Appalachian Magic

Facing Down Extraordinary: A Series of Ordinary Heroes

Hacking Cybercrime: Dana Sanderson Short Mysteries

Passages in the Real World: Six Stories of Life's Transitions

Fantastic Side Trips: Side Characters Take Center Stage

A Kaleidoscope of Cat Tales: Five Stories of Cats and People Who Love Them

Aunties Among Us: Five Tales of Fabulous Women

Four-Legged Heroes: When Pets Rescue People

Anthologies with Jason A. Adams:

Shadows Mountain Deep: Six Appalachian Crime Tales

Uncommon Holidays: A Different Side of the Season

Partnership in Crime: Six Journeys to Justice

ABOUT KARI

Kari and her husband Jason A. Adams met in a computer lab in college in 1990 and proceeded to live out several enduring romance tropes, including rebound romance, friends into lovers, young love, and even second chance romance when they divorced and remarried, all before the end of the 90s. So it was perhaps inevitable that they'd both end up writing romance.

Both coffee and batting cages helped her survive her time in Corporate America with her sanity relatively intact.

Kari writes romance, fantasy, contemporary fiction, mystery, and science fiction, and she's happiest when she surprises herself. She lives with Jason, various house critters, and wildlife they're better off not knowing more about.

The Confidential Adventure Club

For Kari's exclusive free After The End stories and deleted scenes, discounts, early pre-sale releases, adorable pet photos, and a whole lot more not available anywhere else, join us in The Club.

Hope to see you there!

www.KariKilgore.com
www.SpiralPublishing.net
www.ConfidentialAdventureClub.com

BB bookbub.com/authors/kari-kilgore
a amazon.com/author/karikilgore
g goodreads.com/karikilgore
f facebook.com/kari.kilgore.1

www.ingramcontent.com/pod-product-compliance
Lightning Source LLC
Chambersburg PA
CBHW020400110726

47899CB00006B/1789